Last Sam's Cage

Last Sam's Cage

David A. Poulsen

KEY PORTER BOOKS

Library and Archives Canada Cataloguing in Publication

Poulsen, David A., 1946–
      Last Sam's cage / David A. Poulsen.

ISBN 1-55263-611-9

I. Title.

PS8581.O848L37 2004   jC813'.54   C2004-904156-8

The publisher gratefully acknowledges the support of the Canada Council for the Arts
and the Ontario Arts Council for its publishing program. We acknowledge the support
of the Government of Ontario through the Ontario Media Development Corporation's
Ontario Book Initiative.

We acknowledge the financial support of the Government of Canada through the
Book Publishing Industry Development Program (BPIDP) for our publishing activities.

Key Porter Books Limited
70 The Esplanade
Toronto, Ontario
Canada M5E 1R2

www.keyporter.com

Text design: Peter Maher
Electronic formatting: Beth Crane, Heidy Lawrance Associates

Printed and bound in Canada

04 05 06 07 08 09 6 5 4 3 2 1

For Murray, Amy and Brad and their families—my family.
For Mom.
And for Barb.
Always and always.

Acknowledgements

This book would not have happened without the contributions of a number of people. I thank them: Hazel Flewelling, formerly with the Red Deer Young Offender Centre, who first suggested I should write about young offenders; Sergeant Ross Woronka of the Calgary Police Service; Staff Sergeant Verne Fielder of the Calgary Police Service (Youth Unit); Nancy Hills, Programs Supervisor, Calgary Young Offenders Centre; Brian Keating, Head of Conservation Outreach at the Calgary Zoo; Probation Officer/Social Worker Cheryl Brandford; Linda Pruessen, whose wonderfully insightful and sensitive editing added so much to this work; my agent Arnold Gosewich; and finally, Peter Gzowski, who cared about this issue as he did all issues important to Canadians and in his caring, he enlightened . . . and inspired.

Special thanks are due to the Canada Council for the Arts: Writing and Publishing Section for providing a grant that made the writing of this book possible.

Last Sam's Cage

One

It was time.

The house was dark and almost still. Eddie Slater could hear it behind the closed bedroom door, the sleep-breathing of his mother and stepfather. In the quiet of the hallway he noticed that their breaths came almost in unison, and he thought for a moment about how weird this was. His mom and Steve were actually together on something . . . and neither one knew it.

He moved slowly and silently across the carpeted floor, alert to his own fear. He had practiced this walk dozens of times; he even knew how many steps it would take. But even with all the preparation, he hadn't really thought it would happen this way—that he would end up sneaking out of his own house in the dead of night.

But he was right to be going now; he knew that. Steve had threatened him again, threatened to kill him, and Eddie was sure that one day soon, his stepfather would do more than threaten. The move from a beating—one that left bloodstains on the floor and bruises over most of Eddie's body—to actually killing him seemed to Eddie a small one. Yes, it was time to go.

And there was something else that was totally weird. Eddie had broken into dozens of houses—he'd lost count of the B and E's he'd done—but he'd never had to break *out* before. He reached the top of the stairs and shifted his hockey bag on his shoulder. He couldn't afford to lose his balance now. The equipment bag wasn't heavy—there wasn't much in it, just the stuff Eddie thought he'd need. He'd had it packed and buried in his closet for months while he waited for the perfect time to go.

But there had never been a perfect time and there never would be. Now was as good a time as any—if he could just make it to the front door. He went down the stairs one at a time, the way a small child would. Right foot down, then left foot down to meet it. It took longer this way, but Eddie didn't care. It was more important to be sure—and quiet—than to be fast.

Knowing this was one thing, believing it was another. Every few seconds Eddie could feel the panic swelling in him like a deep breath and he was forced to stop and fight it down. He'd never been this scared in his life, not on his first break-in, not even the time he and his buddies had been caught. The people next door had seen them going in through the window and had called the police. The cops were waiting when they came out of the house. But there was a difference—a big difference. Getting caught by the cops was one thing, but if he was caught tonight, Eddie knew he might not be alive in the morning.

He reached the bottom of the stairs and stopped. He shifted the equipment bag again. He wanted it in a different position in case he had to run. Because now he *would* run. Eddie wasn't entirely sure he could outrun Steve, but he also wasn't sure how far Steve would chase him. What if Steve was naked? Eddie almost laughed. But then Steve would get dressed and try to find him in the car and maybe call the police. No, it would definitely be better not to have to run at all.

Seven steps from the bottom of the stairs to the front door. One, two, three . . . Eddie stopped dead in his tracks. He'd heard a noise, from upstairs. Someone was awake. It had to be Steve; Eddie's mother never got up in the night. Eddie figured she was afraid of what might happen if she woke up Steve.

Eddie had to make a decision. He could run and pray for a good lead, or he could crouch down and hope that Steve was just going to the bathroom and wouldn't look down the stairs. He crouched, holding his breath and hoping that the pounding in his chest couldn't be heard at the top of the stairs.

Steve came out of the bedroom wearing only his boxers. Even in the night dark, he looked more like some dangerous animal than a man. Hair covered most of Steve's chest and stomach and even a lot of his back. He was tall, well over six feet, and carried a lot of weight. Not all of it was fat. The man was strong, Eddie knew all about that. Steve belched as he made his way down the hall.

The bathroom was next to Eddie's room. In all the years that Steve had lived in the house he had never looked in on Eddie at night. Still, Eddie couldn't be sure

that this wouldn't be the first time. He breathed a sound-
less sigh of relief when Steve went by his room and into
the bathroom. Steve didn't close the door. Either he
didn't care or he thought the noise of his own water
hitting the bowl was something others should hear. When
he was finished, he didn't bother to flush. Eddie knew it
wasn't because the man didn't want to wake anyone. He
never flushed.

Steve came out of the bathroom and took a few steps
toward the bedroom he shared with Eddie's mother. Then
he stopped. *Was he looking down the stairs?* Eddie closed
his eyes, afraid they might give him away in the dark.
When he dared to open them, Steve was disappearing
into the bedroom. He closed the door noisily behind him.

Eddie exhaled slowly and carefully, but he didn't move.

He would have to wait now. He couldn't risk opening
the front door. In a few seconds Steve would either be
asleep or heaving himself onto Eddie's mother in the noisy,
disgusting ritual that Eddie had often overheard. At first
he'd listened, curious to know the sounds of people making
love. But the sounds he'd heard all those times—he'd
finally concluded that they didn't have anything at all to do
with love. After a while he'd stopped listening. Sometimes,
he even covered his ears.

The minutes ticked by. Finally Eddie could hear the
sleep-breathing again—louder this time and punctuated
by snores. It was time to move. He took the last steps to

the door and set his bag down. He'd need both hands to get the locks undone without waking anyone.

He'd practiced this, too, lots of times and with his eyes closed. He worked by feel. First was the deadbolt. No problem there, he knew, as long as he didn't try to hurry. Next came the lock on the doorknob. His hands found it quickly and easily disengaged it. Now the tricky part—the chain. One hand to slide it back along the groove, the other to lower it down without a sound. As long as he didn't drop it . . . and he didn't.

He hoisted the equipment bag back onto his shoulder and looked up the stairs one last time. No alarming sounds or movement. Eddie turned the handle slowly and eased the door open. He reset the lock and stepped outside, gently closing the door behind him. He was careful to hold the handle until the door was shut. Then he released it, allowing the latch to slide silently back into place. He took a long deep breath of the cold night air. It tasted good. *It tastes like freedom.* Eddie allowed himself a brief smile and set off across the grass—it was quieter than the walk—to the street.

Three blocks away he came to a bus stop and waited in the shadows cast by two tall trees. If the driver thought there was anything strange about a kid with a hockey bag boarding a bus after midnight on a weeknight, he didn't say. There was no one else on the bus and no one at any of the stops for the first while. Eventually an elderly couple got on, then a middle-aged man carrying a really old lunch pail and finally a couple of teenagers. Eddie was glad for the company even though he didn't talk to any of them or look at them after they were in their seats.

Eddie was the first one off. He chose a downtown stop right across from The Bay. It was one of Calgary's busiest corners during the day, but now it was almost deserted. Music was coming from a brightly lit Greek restaurant, but Eddie didn't linger to enjoy it. He wanted to keep moving.

He didn't see the police car until it pulled up to the curb alongside him. One of the cops got out and came toward him. Eddie didn't recognize the guy from any of his previous encounters with Calgary's law enforcement agency. Eddie tried to look casual, like there was nothing to worry about, but he was shaking. He hoped the cop wouldn't notice.

Damn. He was sure Steve had been asleep. What had gone wrong? And how had they found him this fast? The second cop was out of the car now, a few steps behind the first one. They were almost to Eddie. He tried to think of something to say. But he didn't get the chance. The second cop spoke first.

"That's him, over against the wall, must have stumbled this far before he fell."

Eddie looked over his shoulder. A man lay on the pavement, blood oozing from what looked like a wound in his chest. The two cops went quickly past Eddie, one on either side, and knelt next to the man. The first cop stood up again, almost immediately. "I'll call for an ambulance. He's going to need one."

The music from the restaurant got louder. It was a Stones tune. Eddie couldn't remember the name, but judging from the volume someone in the restaurant liked the song a lot. Eddie continued down the street. He didn't look back. When good luck came your way you didn't question it. You just took it.

Turning the corner at Seventh Avenue and heading east, he did something he hadn't done in a long time. As he shifted the equipment bag to his other shoulder, Eddie Slater laughed.

Two

The tiger blinked. It was a slow, lazy blink, almost like she was drifting off to sleep. But after a few seconds, the large careful eyes opened again. And they watched the boy sitting at the picnic table just outside the cat's enclosure.

Eddie Slater was small for fifteen. He was thinner than most boys his age, more pale, too. Brown hair scattered itself haphazardly down over his forehead in the direction of deep-set, serious blue eyes. His face was longish and narrow, with bones that made sharp angles here and there. His chin jutted out over what some of the kids at school called his "pencil neck."

There was a rustling noise behind him. He quickly closed the worn notebook he'd been writing in and stood up, ready to move. The zoo had been closed to the public for a couple of hours and he worried that a security guard on his rounds might be approaching. The noise had come from a cluster of spruce and poplar trees. Eddie clenched his fists nervously as he stared hard at the trees, trying to spot whomever or whatever had been doing the rustling. A magpie, vividly black and white, flapped down from a low branch of one of the poplars and landed on the ground close to Eddie. The bird loudly protested the presence of this stranger, then, apparently satisfied that it had made its feelings known, flew off in a low straight line and disappeared quickly behind other trees.

Eddie relaxed and grinned. He realized his legs were shaking. Gone just over half a day and already his nerves were getting to him. He'd have to get a handle on that. This would be difficult enough without being spooked every time he heard a noise or saw a shadow. He sat back down at the picnic table and opened the notebook again. In the margin next to where he'd been writing earlier he scribbled a note: "First crisis—a stupid magpie. Get a grip!"

He looked up at the mother tiger. For the last while she hadn't paid him any attention. She'd been busy licking her baby and manoeuvring it around with her nose. And she'd yawned a couple of times. But now she was looking intently at him.

"Get used to me," he told her. "I live here now. Been living here for . . . I don't know, maybe four . . . four and a half hours. I guess that makes us neighbours." He waved an arm at the enclosure, the trees and the picnic table. "Nice place you got here."

Eddie looked down at what he'd written. "Want to hear this?" He turned to face the tiger directly. She didn't move, but her baby curled in against her chest and closed its eyes. "Actually, you don't have any choice, because I'm going to read it, anyway."

He pulled the book closer and stared down at the page.

April 19, evening. Last night I escaped. The weird thing is that I escaped to a place where all the residents are locked up. Oh, they're treated real good and everything, but they can't just leave. I know what that's like.

It feels strange to be here. The zoo has been closed for a couple of hours and the only people I've seen since are zookeeper types. I guess they have to have people on duty all the time. And a few security guards are wandering around mostly looking bored.

The tiger looked like she was still paying attention, sort of. "You want to know something strange?" he asked. "At school I hated journal writing. Miss Shackleton, our English teacher, made us write something every day. Most days I didn't feel like writing about my life and stuff, so I just wrote about what TV shows I watched and junk like that.

"After a while that got boring, so I started making stuff up. Like one day, I wrote about this gorgeous twenty-two-year-old blond babe who lived across the street and how she got undressed in front of her upstairs bedroom window every night. I even wrote about how she waved to me and touched her breasts to get me going. None of it was true, but I figured it would add a little excitement to Miss Shackleton's journal reading. Actually, there's an old couple living across the street, Mr. and Mrs. Hunt, and they're okay except Mr. Hunt has Alzheimer's and he's sort of losing it a little.

"Anyway, Miss Shackleton told me I'd have to clean up my act, so I went back to writing about television and the movies. And now here I am . . . writing a journal. Except I'm not going to call it a journal because journals are usually written for teachers. At least the ones you write in school. But this—whatever it's called—isn't for Miss Shackleton."

Eddie looked up at the darkening red sky. "This is for me. That's one thing Miss Shackleton said that I sort of liked. She talked about how the most important part of the writing process is the writing . . . even if nobody but the writer sees what's written. I guess that's how it is for journals and stuff like this. Oh, yeah . . . and Miss Shackleton also talked about how you should consider your audience when you write. Well, *audience*, there it is." He held up the notebook for the tiger to see.

"Ready for some more?"

It's colder than the radio guys said it would be, but they always get it wrong . . . (The dots are for Miss Shackleton. She loves dots. There's a name for them, but I forget what it is. If you wanted a good mark on your journal entry, you didn't write about chicks taking their clothes off and you put in lots of dots so here's some more ......)

The Calgary Zoo. I've been here before. Once was with my grade six class—that was four years ago. I was here last summer, too. Steve brought me. It was the day after he hit me with the iron and then wrapped its cord around my neck. Something in his eyes made it look like he wasn't going to stop choking me. He did though. And the next day he brought me here. The funny thing is, even though I was here with Steve, I still liked the place. It felt . . . safe, I guess, and I remember thinking how great it would be if Steve just sort of forgot to take me home and left me here. Of course, he didn't forget.

I've got a place picked out to sleep in. It's a storage shed where they keep equipment and stuff. I checked it out a little while ago. It was locked, but getting in was easy. I doubt if the security guards bother with the place, and even if they do I can hide behind some of the junk that's piled up in there. It should be okay, at least for a few nights.

He looked up. The mother tiger was still staring at him. It seemed like forever since anyone had listened to anything he had to say for this long. And even though they were just tigers, it was still a nice feeling.

22

Eddie looked away from the cage and for a few minutes didn't say anything. When he spoke, his voice was soft and a little husky.

"We lived in a small town not far from here when I was a kid, a place called Long Prairie. I think my dad wanted to be a farmer but couldn't afford to buy an actual farm. So we lived in that little town so Dad could at least be around farmers. He taught music lessons, too. Once he told me he'd always wanted to be a professional musician, but I guess he never quite made it. He just gave lessons. Sometimes I think it must have been hard to be an almost farmer and an almost musician, but he didn't seem to mind—at least he never said anything.

"We had this beat-up old tent, and every spring—and lots of times even before spring—we'd be off to the mountains camping. We spent some cold nights out there and a few times we had to brush snow off the tent in the morning, but Dad and me, we loved it. I don't think Mom minded it all that much either. On those early-spring camping trips, Dad would cook breakfast. He had a deal with Mom. She cooked breakfast in July and August when it was warm and Dad cooked in what Mom called the winter months, which was all the other months of the year. We spent a lot of time in the outdoors. My dad was pretty good at it and he taught me a lot of stuff. I guess that's why I'm not too worried about staying here by myself, even though it's not exactly camping.

"Then we moved into the city. It had something to do with money. Dad got a job here teaching music. So I guess that's why we came. I don't think my dad wanted to leave Long Prairie. He never laughed as much after that. I mean, we still had fun and everything, but it wasn't the same.

"A couple of years later he died. It was some heart thing he'd had since he was a little kid that he never told anybody about. I went over to my friend's house one Saturday morning and when I came home my dad was dead. I was ten years old then.

"Even though I missed my dad and everything, it wasn't so bad, just Mom and me. She worked long hours at this hotel restaurant, so we didn't see each other that much, but we got along pretty good. I learned to cook not too bad since I had to make all my own meals, but that was okay, too. I was even getting good marks at school.

"Then Mom met Steve and he moved in with us real fast. At first things were all right. He had a good job with the government and Mom got to be at home more, which I liked. Steve yelled a lot and he liked to say things that made you feel stupid, but that was about it. Then he lost his job. He said it was cutbacks, but I think they probably figured out what a jerk he really was. He was around more once he didn't have a job, and that's when I learned all about the real Steve.

"The first time he hit me was when I tried to stop him from pushing Mom around. He was shoving her up against the wall real hard and then when she bounced off the wall, he'd slam her against it again. She was crying and everything so I jumped in to save her like I was Clint Eastwood or somebody. I didn't help much, maybe made things worse. He bounced Mom off the wall a few more times and then gave me a crack across the face that puffed me up so I could only see out of one eye for about a week." Eddie stopped. It hurt to think about that night. But it was sort of good to talk about it, too. Especially like this—with just two tigers listening.

"After that, Steve punching me got to be a regular thing. I guess the part I hated most was that Mom went along with it. She never once stood up for me. Not that first time when I tried to help her or any other time either. I didn't see Steve beat on her anymore, though. Maybe he liked kicking the crap out of me better. Anyway, Mom never said a word to me about any of it. I saw a TV show once that said some women will side with the husband or the boyfriend when he's knocking the kids around because they're afraid of losing the guy. I guess that's how it was for my mom. Or maybe she was just afraid, period.

"I missed quite a bit of school when I was healing up. Steve wouldn't let me go out of the house when I had bruises or cuts showing. Then when I got back to school,

I'd get ragged on by the teachers or the vice-principal for having so many absences.

"Eventually, Steve got pretty good at knowing where to hit. Even yesterday, when I figured he'd totally lost it and might never stop, he didn't go for my face or arms. So just looking at me you'd never know. Unless I took off my shirt. Then you'd know real quick. Except you'd probably think I got hit by a truck. I'm pretty much black from my chest down to just above my knees. I got a bad pain in my side, too. I thought at first he'd busted one of my ribs. But it's not quite as bad right now, so I'm probably okay.

"Anyway, I better get writing." He looked at the tigers. "All the stuff I just told you is going in my notebook."

Eddie stood up and stretched his legs. They were starting to stiffen up as the night temperature dropped.

"I get the same way when it's cold and damp."

The voice was somewhere behind him! And not far away. Eddie whirled around, his heart pounding so hard he thought it might break through his chest.

Three

At first Eddie couldn't see anyone. Then, slowly, a figure moved out of the shadows. It was a man; an old man, or at least *older*.

"Shit! You nearly gave me a heart attack," Eddie said, watching the man closely, his mind spinning ideas around in his head. *If he comes any closer, do I run or hit him? Hit him with what—a notebook? Yeah, right.*

"Go ahead, finish your story. I'd like to hear the rest."

"I don't think so."

"Why not?" The man chuckled a little. "If I'd wanted to mug you, I could have done it while you were talking to the tigers or writing in your book."

Eddie stared at the man, not caring if he was being rude. After all, he wasn't the one who'd been listening in on a private conversation. It was hard to figure the guy's age, but Eddie guessed fifties, maybe sixty. He was wearing okay clothes, not like some derelict. The jeans had some age on them, but they weren't ratty. His jacket was the plain-looking zipper-up-the-front type a lot of men that age seemed to wear. It was unzipped now and hanging open. Beneath it was a Calgary Stampede sweatshirt with a picture of a bucking bronc. His running shoes weren't in much better shape than Eddie's. He was wearing a plain blue ball cap, and there were patches of greyish hair sticking out in a couple of places.

It was the man's face that made him look old. It was thin—sort of hollow-looking—and it sagged a little under the eyes. The rest of him wasn't skinny like his face, but it wasn't fat either. Even though the guy wasn't real big—at least not like he spent his spare time lifting weights—Eddie had a feeling he wasn't some weak old man. Eddie had seen enough tough guys—and lots who talked tough but weren't—to know that this wasn't some-body who got pushed around a lot.

He was tall, too, which probably added to the feeling that there wasn't much to him. Definitely not a cop, Eddie decided. But that face. Eddie looked at him again. The face—so skinny and sad-looking—made the old guy look fairly harmless.

Still, looks can fool you sometimes and Eddie couldn't afford to be fooled. He decided to be very careful, espe-cially since the guy already knew more about him than he wanted anybody to know.

The man stepped forward, moving slowly like he knew Eddie didn't trust him. He stuck out his hand. "Jack Simm."

Eddie ignored the hand. He wasn't about to tell this stranger his name, either. Hell, the guy could be a pervert.

It was like Jack Simm read his mind. "Don't worry, kid. Little boys aren't my thing."

He sat down at the picnic table. "Look, if we're going to be neighbours, you might as well finish your life story.

28

Go ahead, tell the tigers if you want. I'll just sit here and listen."

"What do you mean . . . neighbours? You work here?" Eddie asked.

"Nope."

"Well, what did you mean then?"

"I spend some time here, that's all."

"The zoo is closed now." Eddie didn't know why he'd said it but wasn't sure what else to say.

"Yeah." The man shrugged.

"You're not supposed to be here after hours."

"Neither are you."

Eddie watched him. Jack Simm. He looked like somebody who'd be called Jack Simm. Right now all Eddie wanted was for Jack Simm to leave him alone.

"Look, kid, I know you ran away and you're thinking of living here for a while. I figure we might as well get along."

"You . . . live here?"

"Not exactly. But I come here a lot. I guess I know this place better than anybody. So anything you need to know, just ask."

"I don't need your help."

"Maybe . . . maybe not. We'll see how it goes in the next few days. In the meantime, you were saying you've been here before. That's why you chose the place?"

Eddie nodded slowly.

"Probably not a bad choice, actually. How long you planning to stay?"

Jack Simm wasn't going to leave, at least not right away. Eddie could see that. Maybe if he told him a little, the man would be satisfied and go away.

"I'm not sure. I just took off last night, so I haven't had a chance to think about it yet. I mean, you know, I'd been planning to get out of there for a long time, but it's different once you actually do it."

He hadn't intended to say that much, but for some reason it hadn't felt all that bad talking to a real person.

"You have any money?"

"I've got some money," Eddie said. There was no way he was going to tell Jack Simm he had twenty-four bucks and a little change.

"They gonna be looking for you?"

Eddie shrugged. "I figure I've got a couple of days before I have to worry about being seen. It'll be at least that long before Steve and my mom figure out I'm gone. I guess you could say they don't notice me a lot. And once they realize I'm not around they'll think I just stayed over at one of my friends' places. Then Steve . . . that's my step . . . oh yeah, you heard all this . . ."

Jack nodded.

"Well, anyway, Steve, he'll look around and notice I'm not there. Then he'll yell, 'Goddammit, where's that kid?'"

"You better be careful," Jack said softly. "If security sees someone your age hanging around, they'll get curious."

Eddie knew it was good advice. If the security guards called the cops, he'd be back home with the iron cord around his neck. And this time Steve might not let off.

"I'll be careful."

"You travel light." Jack looked at Eddie's bag.

"I guess I didn't think I'd need a lot of stuff." That was an understatement. He had a bag of clothes, mostly T-shirts, jeans and socks—no sweaters. He shivered as if to remind himself that at least one sweater would have been a good idea.

"I guess it's easier to take off if you live in Vancouver," Eddie said.

"I guess so," Jack Simm stood up. "I'll see you, kid." He turned and disappeared through the trees. Eddie heard his footsteps grow fainter as he walked away.

It was weird. Eddie had wanted the guy to leave, but now that he was gone it seemed a lot more lonely. And why had he left then? They were having an okay conversation and suddenly the man just up and disappeared. *Very bizarre.*

Eddie didn't like that Jack Simm knew he was here. He wasn't sure how much Jack had heard, but he guessed the man probably knew where he was planning to sleep. That wasn't good.

Eddie looked at the tigers. The baby was sleeping. The mother was still watching him. "You wouldn't have a sandwich kicking around in there, would you? I'm getting hungry. Doesn't *have* to be a sandwich. Just whatever you've got around. . . . I didn't think so. I suppose I could check out the garbage containers. This afternoon I saw a few people throw away some pretty decent-looking stuff. Thing is, I don't know if I can eat other people's garbage. I guess I probably will when I get hungry enough, but I'm not ready for that just yet, you know what I mean?

"Actually, I kind of like the idea of being here. It beats the street. Last night I just walked around downtown and hung out in an all-night restaurant and then a laundromat. Not fun. And sleeping in doorways or breaking into empty warehouses with fifteen other guys doesn't do it for me. I guess a storage shed isn't much better, but at least it's *my* storage shed. Of course, I might change my mind about living at the zoo come next winter. But that's a long way off. Who knows? Something great might happen between now and then. Maybe I'll be living somewhere decent. I might have a job, which would be cool. I could get an apartment and a car. Or maybe I'll meet a woman. Yeah, she'll have money and she'll take me in to live in this real nice condo and she won't let me get any sleep at night because she's so nuts about my body. Yeah, dream on."

Eddie stamped his feet on the ground. "One thing I'm real sure of—I'm freezing my butt off. It's time to shut down this stimulating conversation we've got going."

The baby tiger opened its eyes, climbed unsteadily to its feet, turned around twice and flopped down again. It burrowed its head into its mother's stomach and started to suck. It was a noisy eater. Eddie waved a small good-bye to the tigers and headed off in the direction of the storage shed.

Four

One week to the day after he arrived at the zoo Eddie decided it was time to get out for a night. Even a person who doesn't mind being alone needs to talk to something that talks back once in a while. Jack Simm hadn't been around since that first night and Eddie wanted to be with creatures that had the same number of legs as he did.

It was also time to test his sneaking-in-and-out technique. There was no point staying at the zoo in a permanent sort of way if he couldn't come and go whenever he wanted.

The getting-out part went fine. A couple of days before, he'd found a perfect break in the chain-link fence. It was just big enough for someone his size. No one saw him leave, which was good because he didn't like the idea of some weirdo finding his secret entrance. One of the best things about the zoo was that once it was closed to the public, the only people Eddie ever saw were the staff. And as far as he knew, they hadn't seen him.

He decided to celebrate—it was sort of an anniversary, one week of freedom—with a cheeseburger and a chocolate shake. He'd been eating a lot of soup, mostly because it was the cheapest thing at the concession, but now he was really looking forward to something that didn't have vegetables floating in it.

He went to a hamburger place just outside the zoo gates. It looked as if it had been there a long time and wasn't improving with age, but Eddie felt like he was eating at the fanciest place in town. He made himself chew slowly, the way they tell people to in those ads for losing weight. It was the best meal he'd had in a long time.

When he finished the burger and fries, he picked up the rest of the shake and wandered in the direction of Chinatown. He had a couple of friends there. In fact, Charlie Chen was probably Eddie's best friend and he figured he owed it to Charlie to let him know what was going on. Eddie hadn't told anyone about his plans to run away before he actually did it, partly because he was afraid that his mom and Steve would find out and partly because he didn't want to look like a jerk if he chickened out at the last minute. But now that he was a real-live runaway it was time to let Charlie in on it.

Eddie knew he'd have to be careful. He was positive Steve and his mom would have reported him to the cops by now. If he got caught he'd be back home before the night was out. One of the rules of his probation was that he had to live at home. Eddie laughed every time he thought about that. Better to be at home where you might get killed than to run away. Yeah, that made sense. Anyway, the cops could be watching Charlie's place and Eddie wasn't about to let himself be caught.

Charlie wasn't his real name. It was Kenny, but he was called Charlie after an old Chinese-movie detective. There was a Charlie Chan movie on TV one night and some of the kids had seen it. By the time school got out the next day, Kenny Chen was Charlie and had been ever since. The nickname had surprised Eddie. Well, actually, the surprising part was that Kenny Chen was okay with it. If he hadn't been, Eddie was pretty sure nobody would have dared use the name. Charlie was somebody you didn't mess with.

Charlie lived in an apartment over a dumpy grocery and restaurant on Center Street that looked like it could fall down if a decent breeze came along. Eddie remembered telling Charlie that somebody should knock the place down before it caved in or caught fire or something.

"They'll never do that." Charlie shook his head. "The place has history. Dr. Sun Yat-sen came to Calgary back in 1910 or so and spoke to all the Chinese people in the city right in this building."

"Who?"

"Dr. Sun Yat-sen. He was a Chinese revolutionary, a hero to our people."

Charlie got kind of excited when he talked about the guy.

Eddie thought it was strange that Charlie had even heard of Dr. Sun Yat-sen. And it was stranger still that Charlie cared about some guy, hero or not, who gave a speech a million years ago in the building where he lived.

All Eddie had ever seen Charlie get excited about was action movies, the kind where thirty or forty people get killed off in the first ten minutes. So this was different, all right. But Eddie always figured it would be better not to say too much about it. Charlie wasn't much fun to be around when he was mad. There were stories around school that Charlie was tight with one of the Asian gangs that hung out a few blocks north of Chinatown. Eddie didn't know one way or the other. Even though they were pretty good friends, it wasn't something they talked about. The only thing he did know was that everybody—even the tough guys at school—cut Charlie a lot of slack.

Eddie stuck mostly to side streets and back alleys on the way to Charlie's place. He stood in the shadows across the street from Charlie's building for a long time. When he was sure that no cops were around, he crossed the street and went around to the back. The stairs looked like they'd been stuck to the outside of the building with Krazy Glue. When he got to the top, there was no screen door, only a wooden one with most of the finish gone.

He knocked. Charlie's sister, Linda, came to the door. Linda was a total hottie in grade nine. Eddie had thought a few times about asking her out but gave up on the idea mostly because he was sure she'd say no. Eddie knew that some girls liked being asked out by older guys, but not guys who looked like him. So he'd never asked. No sense going out of your way to get blown off.

"Kenny's not here," Linda told him and then invited him in. "You want a Coke or anything, a coffee?"

"No thanks. I was just wandering around and figured I'd stop in and see Char . . . Kenny. You know where he is?" Eddie didn't think he should sit down. He didn't want Linda to get the idea he'd be hard to get rid of.

"Probably at the Castle." Linda smiled more or less in Eddie's direction. He liked the way the corners of her eyes wrinkled up. In fact, there wasn't a whole lot about Linda Chen he didn't like. He'd just started to think that sitting down might not be such a bad idea after all when the phone rang. Linda left the room to answer it, which gave Eddie a chance to look around. He'd never been in the place before. Charlie always met him somewhere or made him wait in the alley at the bottom of the stairs.

He noticed the smell of Chinese food; no big surprise since the restaurant was right below. It was an okay smell, but he wasn't sure he'd like to live with it all the time. Except for the smell there wasn't a whole lot about the place that seemed Chinese. The furniture wasn't that different from what he'd seen in most of his friends' houses except that this stuff was older-looking.

There was a brown couch that was worn through in a couple of places. The room had a lot of stuff in it but only one table—a short, wide one that stood in the corner next to the TV. There were things on the table that really did look Chinese. Instead of the usual books and ceramic horses and pictures, this table held four carvings, maybe porcelain. There were three old Chinese men in flowing robes, and in the centre of the table was a small building. He wasn't sure what kind of building it was, maybe a temple or something. It had lots of layers, like a fountain or one of those cakes they display in bakery windows. Eddie liked the little building. He thought he might ask Linda about it when she came back.

He noticed something else, too. Even though some of the furniture looked as if it was ready to collapse from age and wear, the room was clean, real clean. In fact, it looked like Linda had been cleaning just before he got there. A broom and dustpan were leaning against the wall and there was a lemonish smell in the room. The lemon smell mixed in with the smell of the Chinese food. It wasn't a nice mix.

He was still looking at the stuff on the table when Linda came back. "You can sit down, you know," she smiled.

He looked down at his feet. He did that sometimes, he wasn't sure why, maybe to warn them: *Don't go clumsy on me right now*. He walked over to the couch and sat down, careful to avoid a spring that was poking through. "Uh . . . thanks . . . so how's everything going?" He wished he could have come up with something a little more exciting to say, but every time he looked at Linda it was like his communication skills disappeared.

"Okay," she answered. "What about you? I haven't seen you around school for a while."

"They . . . uh . . . didn't have any announcements or anything about me not being there?"

"No . . . why would they?"

"Uh . . . no reason." Eddie was relieved. If Steve and his mom *were* looking for him, they hadn't gone to the cops, at least not yet. Cops would've made announcements on the P.A. at school. Eddie had heard them when other kids were gone for a while. Maybe Steve was afraid to go to the cops. Maybe he figured if somebody saw the bruises on Eddie's body, he might be in more trouble than Eddie.

"I . . . I've been visiting my aunt over in Bridgeland. She's sick." He didn't like lying to Linda, but at least Bridgeland was not far from the zoo so maybe the lie wasn't *that* bad. He didn't know why he'd lied to her at all. It didn't really matter if Linda knew he'd taken off. Maybe she'd even think it was cool. Anyway, it was too late. He'd said it; he'd have to go with it now.

"So, when are you coming back?"

"Pretty soon, I guess." Suddenly Eddie wanted out of there. For one thing, he didn't want to hear himself lie anymore and there was no telling how much more B.S. he'd have to throw out now that he'd started. "Uh, maybe I'll wander over to the Castle and see if Charlie's there." He didn't bother to correct himself this time. Linda must have heard her brother's nickname.

"Yeah," she said. That was another thing about Linda Chen. She had a great voice, sort of husky and low. She could make a word like "yeah" do interesting things inside your head. He tried to imagine what it would be like to kiss her—long and slow and sexy—and then afterwards to hear that voice saying, "Eddie, that was so great."

Yeah, right. He stood up and turned to go, but before he got to the door, Linda said, "Maybe I'll come along with you. I need to get out of here for a while."

Eddie swallowed a couple of times. First of all, girls like Linda didn't usually hang out at arcades, not even excellent ones like the Castle. And he didn't figure she'd be into watching her brother shoot pool and smoke cigarettes. So that meant Linda Chen wanted to go for a walk—with him, Eddie Slater, on a public street where people, real people, might see them together. His mind started going real fast. *Jeez, I've spent the last few nights sleeping in a storage shed. I haven't had a shower in a week and my clothes probably look like zoo animals have been dancing on them. This isn't how I pictured my first date with Linda Chen. But, of course, it isn't really a date.*

While Linda was getting her coat, Eddie checked himself out in a mirror that was hanging on a door, a closet maybe. Face . . . hair . . . no better or worse than normal. Clothes, not bad—not bad at all considering where they'd been. The shoes were the worst. They were gross, with mud splotches and grass stains covering the parts that used to be white. He swore at himself for not cleaning them up before he got here. Oh, well. Nothing he could do about it now. He'd just have to hope Linda didn't spend a lot of time looking down.

She came back wearing one of those fake-suede jackets. Even the fake version probably cost more than everything Eddie had taken when he left home. She looked great. He held the door for her, but she motioned him out first so she could lock it. On the way to the arcade, they mostly talked about cars. Linda was interested in hot cars—Porsches, Jags, BMWs. *Yeah, no problem there, Linda. I'll just pick you up next Friday night in the Testarosa and we'll do cocktails and dinner.*

Eddie was beginning to think he fit in better at the zoo. At least with the animals, he didn't have to put on an act and try to be somebody he wasn't. The thing about zebras and rhinos and all the rest—they didn't really care what your shoes looked like, or what kind of car you drove.

"What kind of movies do you like?" He was hoping to get off the topic of high-performance cars.

"Oh, you know, Jean-Claude Van Damme, Arnold Schwarzenegger. And I really liked the Charlie's Angels movies."

"Yeah, me too," he lied. Again. He hoped she wouldn't get into any details. Eddie had only seen a couple of action-movie videos that Steve brought home and he thought they were pretty stupid. Not that he'd say that to Linda. All that crap about being yourself? Eddie figured that might be okay if the self you were being was a whole lot cooler than he was.

"What about *You've Got Mail*? You like that one?" He only asked the question because he'd read somewhere that it was a chick flick. He hadn't seen it yet, but it sounded better than five or six Charlie's Angels sequels.

"God, wasn't that dumb?" Linda laughed. "All those love movies just kill me. They are *so* unbelievable. And stupid."

"Uh . . . yeah, totally stupid," he agreed. The evening wasn't going well, no doubt about that. Eddie had started to think that he and Linda might not have much of a future together.

They got to the arcade and though the place was packed, Charlie wasn't there. Eddie played a couple of games of Atomic Punk 2 and on the second game racked up a score of 37,000 points. The screen said it was the second-highest score ever, but Linda didn't seem to notice.

They were getting ready to leave, when a big guy with a mohawk and a pathetic attempt at a Fu Manchu moustache stepped in front of them. He was wearing a muscle shirt and smoking a cigarette and he blew a cloud of smoke in their faces. Eddie didn't recognize him right away—maybe it was the bad moustache. Then he remembered. The guy had been in the Calgary Young Offenders Centre at the same time as Eddie. Eddie didn't know much about him, but he'd heard lots; most of it bad. The guy's name was Stink something . . . Pender or Parker, Eddie wasn't exactly sure. What he *was* sure about was that Stink had a reputation as somebody who didn't mind hurting people just for fun. In fact, Stink was in the CYOC because he'd beaten the crap out of some kid for laughing at one of his answers in English class. The kid needed major surgery to rebuild his face. Stink wasn't in the CYOC long and Eddie—and just about everyone else—was real happy when he left.

But for Eddie, Stink's departure came one day too late. A bunch of kids had been playing basketball in the gymnasium. Eddie and Stink were on opposing teams. The whole thing was weird because in the entire time he was in the place, Eddie had never once played basketball.

It wasn't much of a game. Stink's team was winning big and Stink had scored most of the points. Right near the end of the game, Eddie and Stink got tangled up. Eddie came away with the ball and actually scored. Eddie was jumping around celebrating, because for him baskets were almost as rare as girlfriends. The next thing he knew, he was on his back with Stink's big hands around his throat. He was having trouble getting air by the time the guards and a teacher got Stink off him.

"Do that again, you piece of shit, and I'll rip that joke you call a face—" That was as far as Stink got before the guards hauled him out of the gymnasium.

And now here they were—Stink who went psycho when somebody showed him up and Eddie who had done the showing. Had Stink remembered him? So far, Eddie didn't think so—mostly because Stink hadn't noticed him at all. The creep's attention was totally on Linda. He was grinning at Linda, his cigarette still in his mouth.

Eddie realized that he was scared. Stink gave a person lots to be scared about. He was a year or two older than Eddie and at least a head taller. He had tattoos on both arms—lightning bolts and naked women seemed to be Stink's favourite themes. He had a pool cue in his hands and he was carrying it so that it blocked the way out. Yeah, Eddie was scared. He couldn't tell, but he figured Linda was scared, too.

Eddie noticed that the arcade was suddenly a lot less noisy. The smoke was still there, hanging at about eye level, and it was still crowded. But it was quieter now. And there wasn't as much moving around. It was like the whole place was watching to see what would happen.

"Hey, babe," Stink said, still looking at Linda, "it's about time you and me . . ." He made an obscene gesture that wasn't too hard to figure out.

Now Eddie was sure Linda was scared. She hadn't said or done anything, but she didn't need to. You can tell when somebody is scared. She moved a little closer to him.

Yeah, like I'm going to protect you from Stink the Wacko.

"Take a hike," Linda told Stink. It was about what you'd expect somebody to say in this situation, but it wasn't real effective. Linda's voice wasn't helping her out. She hadn't actually squeaked, but it was pretty close.

Eddie couldn't take his eyes off Stink. It's weird how sometimes you can't stop looking at somebody, even if he's one of the biggest jerks going. Watching him, Eddie was sure Stink thought Linda actually wanted him. Guys like him usually think that way.

Stink reached out and rubbed his hand up and down Linda's arm. This time her voice worked just fine. "Hands off, dirtbag."

"Hey, baby, you're my woman." Stink grinned at her. It didn't help his overall appearance. There was nothing but air where a couple of teeth should have been. That surprised Eddie. He'd heard that Stink came from a wealthy family—Pagler, that was his last name, Stink Pagler. Real wealthy. In fact, the word at the CYOC was that it was Daddy's money that got Stink out so fast. You'd think if this was true, his old man could have invested a little of that cash in something to fill the gaps in his kid's mouth.

"You and me both know it's gonna happen." Stink leaned closer to Linda. "Either way, you can love it or fight it, but I'm going to have a real good time on that nice little body of yours . . ." As he was talking, Stink reached out and touched Linda again. Only this time it wasn't on the arm.

Afterwards, when he thought about it, Eddie decided that what happened next must have been caused by malnutrition. The burger and fries was the first actual meal he'd eaten in about three days. He'd heard that not eating enough can make you light-headed. Or maybe it was all those bad sleeps in the storage shed. Whatever the reason, he lost it. Eddie kicked Stink Pagler between the legs. The five hole. Bull's eye. Direct hit. Like a place-kicker putting one through the goalposts.

That was probably what saved them—the kick being a perfect shot. Stink crumpled up like tissue in a campfire and fell to the floor. But even lying on the floor holding himself and making sucking noises, Stink was dangerous. He puked. Eddie had to move fast because Stink had puked in the direction of his shoes. Dirt and grass stains were one thing, but Eddie drew the line at Stink vomit.

As he was rolling around on the floor, Stink looked up at Eddie through water-clouded eyes. In a way it was almost funny. *Well, at least he's finally noticed me*, Eddie thought. He looked down at the writhing figure on the arcade floor. Stink Pagler with missing teeth and puke running down his hairy chin and a face that hated as much as somebody can hate wasn't a real pretty picture.

"You . . . again." Stink said it in a voice that Eddie could barely hear. Stink tried to get up on one knee, but he slumped back on the floor, his eyes never leaving Eddie's face. "You're one dead bastard." Even with pain all through them, Stink's words scared the crap out of Eddie. Because he knew that if Stink ever got the chance, he'd make those words come true.

Eddie felt Linda pulling at his arm. He didn't need a lot of coaxing. They stepped around Stink Pagler and ran into the street. They turned right and didn't stop running until they were four blocks from the arcade. They leaned against the brick wall of a building, pressing their chests like that might help get some oxygen back into their burning lungs. Eddie slid down the wall until he was sitting on the pavement. After a while he was able to breathe a little better. He looked up and watched the neon sign of a furniture store flashing on and off. It was as if all his senses were on zoom. Somewhere close by there was a smell that was familiar. It was like the garage of his parents' house in Long Prairie—a combination of grease and wet cloths. At least it seemed like that.

Linda spoke first. "Shit."

"Yeah."

"I think he meant it . . . about you being dead."

"Probably." Eddie nodded. He wondered why Linda felt it necessary to remind him of Stink's threat. It wasn't like Eddie was going to forget, at least not for quite a while.

"I'm pretty sure Stink Pagler could kill someone if he hated them enough." Linda looked at him.

Eddie let his head slump forward and stared at a chunk of the pavement.

"You didn't have to do that, you know," Linda said.

He looked up at her. "Oh, really? Well, it looked to me like I had to do something and I was a little short of ideas at that exact moment. And thanks for cheering me up like this."

"I mean . . . like, thanks."

Eddie tilted his head back so that it rested against the cool brick of the building. It felt good. Linda was fumbling around in her purse.

"You got a cigarette?"

Eddie shook his head as he watched her. He had just risked his life for a woman who liked Arnold Schwarzenegger better than she liked Tom Hanks. He stood up. "We better get going. I'm not sure how long sore gonads will keep Stink from forming a posse and coming after us."

They started running again. When they got to Linda's house the goodbyes were short. "You'd better tell your brother about this," Eddie advised. "He should be able to keep Stink under control."

"I'm not the one with the problem. He only wants to have sex with me. He wants to kill you."

"I wish you wouldn't keep bringing that up."

Eddie went back to the zoo using the same alleys and side streets he'd travelled earlier that night. He arrived with all his parts still attached. He would never have believed that the storage shed could actually look good, but just then it was about the most inviting piece of architecture he'd ever seen. He didn't expect his sleep that night to be any better than all the rest, but at least it wasn't the big sleep—the knife-in-the-guts kind.

Eddie lay on his cardboard mattress for quite a while trying to decide if the evening had been a success or not. He fell asleep before he made up his mind.

Five

Eddie stood in the Reptile Building looking through a piece of glass at a boa constrictor. The glass needed cleaning, but it didn't matter because there wasn't a whole lot to watch. Compared to the snake, the Siberian tiger mother and cub were party animals. Eddie had been standing in front of the enclosure for at least three-quarters of an hour and so far the boa constrictor hadn't moved.

The snake wasn't the reason he was there. He was trying to warm up after another night in the storage shed. Last night had been cold—colder even than the night he'd arrived at the zoo. The walls of the shed were pretty well useless at keeping out the wind that had blown most of the night. He had slept maybe an hour in total.

Things hadn't improved much with the arrival of morning. He couldn't make his body stop shivering. He turned away from the snake and looked at his reflection in a second pane of glass. This one was cleaner. It was the front wall of an enclosure for something called a Tokay gecko, but the gecko either wasn't home or was very good at hiding. Eddie stared at himself for a while. It wasn't something he liked doing. Not that he was gross-looking exactly. But he couldn't imagine anyone thinking of him as handsome either. If there was a category for people like him, Eddie figured it was the "nobody notices you" category.

It wasn't a complaint. Eddie didn't really mind his looks except that they lacked chick appeal. And even that seemed to matter a lot more to everybody else than it did to him. The acne did bug him, but there wasn't a lot he could do about it except for those dumb products they were always advertising. He preferred the acne to going into a store and suffering the embarrassment of actually buying any of that stuff.

Sometimes he wished he was bigger—maybe more of a jock. That was what the girls at school seemed to go for. All that sensitive-guy stuff was crap. If you played quarter-back and looked like you should be in a daytime soap, your chick problems were over. He'd spent a lot of time the year before learning the side-to-side rolling walk of the school's athletes. They all did it—it was part of the package. He got pretty good at it and after a while figured anybody watching him walk would think "jock" right off. The problem was after, when he stopped walking and actually had to go into the gym and *play* some sport. Then his athlete impersonation sort of blew up. If you had to dribble it, shoot it, pass it, hit it, throw it or kick it, Eddie Slater was in trouble. *Except for that one deadly accurate kick. But maybe that didn't count, since it wasn't actually in a game.*

The reflection in the glass reminded him that his hair was also a problem. It was browner than usual because it needed a wash. He ran a comb through it, but it didn't help.

He followed the reflection back down to his face. He'd never been able to figure out who he looked more like, his mom or his dad. His face was like his dad's, at least the way Eddie remembered him. Except for the eyes. Eddie's eyes were blue and they wrinkled up when he smiled and that part was more like his mom. Though neither of them smiled often anymore, it seemed.

"I thought you were supposed to look fatter in a mirror," he said out loud. He didn't look fat. Quite the opposite. Some of the kids at school—the same ones who'd come up with "pencil neck"—made sure Eddie didn't forget that skinny was probably the most noticeable thing about him.

"Hey, Slater, somebody could drink Slurpees through your arms."

"I've seen fettuccine noodles that are thicker than your wrists."

"You ever hear of something called muscles, Slater?"

Muscles, now *there* was a joke. To have muscles you had to have flesh and Eddie didn't have much going for him in that department. What Eddie did have going for him was mostly bones, hair and pockmarks. The funny part was that neither of his parents were skinny. He turned away from the glass. He'd already spent more time than he usually did checking himself out. He wasn't big on standing in front of the bathroom mirror. He figured people like him were probably happy to get that part of their day over with in a hurry.

He hadn't really thought about bathrooms until that moment. He realized suddenly they were something you had to think about, especially when there wasn't one just down the hall. Oh, there were lots of toilets around, no problem there. But zoos don't come with showers and Eddie liked to be clean. Even if you weren't much to look at, you didn't have to smell bad. There were guys at school who needed to be reminded about that—he couldn't believe it some days.

He'd have to figure something out in the personal-hygiene department pretty soon or he'd be just as bad. Hitting the river was not an option, at least not for a while. There were still ice chunks floating here and there. Eddie had always hated the cold. He couldn't stand winter, even if it was kind of pretty sometimes. That was why he'd waited until now to run away. He didn't like the idea of living outside during a nasty prairie winter. And the winter that had just concluded had been one of the nastiest in years—at least that's what the paper had said.

He shivered again. Maybe he should have waited a little longer before taking off. His dad had always said you could never be sure of spring in this country until summer. Trouble was, the longer Eddie stayed in that house, the better the chances were that he was going to get hurt real bad; he was sure of that.

Even so, if spring didn't roll in soon, Eddie was sure he'd wind up with pneumonia or some other cold-weather disease. He didn't know if there were actually diseases you could get just from being cold, but if there were he figured he'd have most of them by noon.

The snake moved. Not a big move, more of a sigh than anything else. Did snakes sigh? It reminded Eddie that he needed to move around himself. He was stiff from the cold. He walked back and forth a few times in front of the long row of enclosures. The zoo was open now, but it was still early. He thought about whether it was a good idea to leave the building and decided against it. Better to wait until there were more people around.

He paced a while longer, then decided to work on his next journal entry. There was no picnic table in the reptile building so he sat down cross-legged on the floor. He pulled the notebook out of his backpack and leaned against the wall across from a pair of salamanders. He stared at the page for a long time and when he finally did write something it was only one line.

It wasn't like he had writer's block or anything. He just wasn't sure how he wanted to say the next part. He didn't really want to say it at all, but he figured if this was going to be a record of his whole life he had to put everything in. For a while he just thought about it, remembering how it all happened and what it was like. The line he had written read: "I'm a young offender."

The way things were in the world that was like announcing you had joined the Ku Klux Klan. He'd even been in jail. Of course, they didn't call it jail. They gave it a nicer name: the CYOC, which sounded like some church camp if you didn't know it stood for Calgary Young Offenders Centre. But it was jail, all right. You couldn't get out, you were watched all the time and at night you went into your room and the door was closed and locked. He hated that place.

He said the words out loud, slowly, giving each word its own sound, its own meaning. "I'm a young offender."

There was another sound. He heard it right after he had said the word "offender." At first he thought it was one of the reptiles—it was kind of a scratching, shuffling noise. But it wasn't one of the reptiles. Someone was coming around the corner. It was too late—there was no place to go . . . no place to hide. Eddie thought of Stink Pagler. Could Stink have found him this fast? He tried to recall the night before—he'd been sure no one had followed him.

Maybe it was one of the zoo staff. Maybe if he shot past whomever it was he could outrun him. The security guys didn't look as if they were in great shape. Eddie got to his feet and waited for his chance.

"You're going to have to be more careful, kid," the voice said before the speaker even came into view. "If I keep stumbling onto you, eventually someone else will."

Jack Simm came slowly around the corner. "Morning," he said.

Eddie didn't answer. Jack Simm hadn't *stumbled* onto anything, Eddie knew that. But how had he found him? It didn't make sense that this old man kept showing up in places Eddie happened to be.

"You following me or what?" Eddie noticed that the old man had changed his clothes. He had a heavier coat on now, the kind Eddie wished he had right about now. Jack was carrying a paper bag under one arm. *I bet he picks bottles*, Eddie thought.

"Not really." Jack shrugged. "I'm just observant, is all."

"I don't like people following me." Eddie tried to sound tougher than he felt.

"So call a cop." Jack leaned carelessly against the wall.

Eddie didn't answer. Maybe his silence would eventually drive the old man away. They looked at each other for a long minute.

"I don't mind listening, kid."

"Yeah, well, I don't feel like talking to you."

"Really?" Jack shrugged again. "It seems to me that somebody who talks to tigers and reptiles and writes to himself in a book maybe wants to talk to somebody."

"Well, I guess you're wrong."

"My mistake. I'll see you around." Jack turned and walked back around the corner.

Eddie didn't move. He wanted to look around the corner to see if the old man was really gone, but he didn't. It was weird, but he wasn't sure he really wanted Jack to be gone. Maybe there was even a part of him that was actually hoping he'd stopped a little way down the hall.

Eddie sat back down and looked at his notebook again. And after a while he wrote. He wrote slowly and stopped often to think about what he wanted to write next. A couple of times he thought he'd stop. But each time he wanted to quit, he'd close his eyes for a while, then open them and write some more.

April 27, morning. I'm a young offender. We were pathetic when it came to being criminals—more like the Three Stooges. We were hanging out at the 7-Eleven one night, which was pretty much what we did every night. One of the guys was practicing ollies on his skateboard. We were watching him and talking and smoking.

There was a car in the parking lot. It was running and had its lights on and nobody was in it. We made up our minds in about a second and a half. We piled in and took off. We figured this was going to be a hell of an adventure. It was . . . for maybe ten minutes. I still can't believe we got caught that fast.

We figured we'd better stay on the side streets. And that wasn't a bad idea except here comes a police car going the other way. Everybody's going, "It's okay, it's okay, everybody just look natural." Of course, we didn't know the two cops were listening to a description of the stolen car—our stolen car—as they were going by. And then, just to make sure the cops didn't miss us, Cam Kilger, who was driving, went through a stop sign and almost hit a green Chevy half-ton. The driver laid on the horn so long every cop in town probably heard it. The two that had just gone by sure did.

Eddie stopped writing and laughed out loud. He always laughed when he thought about that night. The sound echoed up and down the empty corridor of the Reptile Building. A real bunch of crooks they had been. Yeah, gangsters all the way.

When the cops pulled us over, I was so scared I almost pissed my pants. I had good reason to be scared—not of the cops or even going to court (we were first-time offenders and all we got was community service and probation). No, it was Steve. That time it was a belt. When it didn't seem to be doing as much damage as he wanted it to, he turned it around and used the end with the buckle. Steve likes to wear buckles the size of garbage-can lids. He told me he'd won them all in line-dancing contests.

That wasn't the last car we stole. I think it was the excitement that we liked. It's not like we needed the cars or anything. Teddy Neilson was sixteen and he could get his dad's car anytime he wanted. Teddy was sort of our leader and we followed him around like puppies. And we all liked it when he did show up driving his old man's car. But there was something about knowing we were breaking the law that was . . . very cool. We talked about it sometimes—why we did stuff—but nobody could ever say exactly how or why it was cool. It just was. Of course, for me there was something else. It was a chance to stick something up Steve's you-know-what. That made it even better.

We were smarter after that first time. For one thing we never let Cam drive again. Then we moved on to B and E's. We did about a dozen before we got caught. The cops connected us to two other break-ins, and that time we got three months in custody and more probation.

That's when I got my introduction to the CYOC. I learned to hate it real fast. But the thing I remember most about being in there wasn't the place at all. It was a guy named Ratsy. I'll never forget Ratsy. I still don't know his real name; Ratsy was all I ever heard him called. He was the same age as me and somebody told me he was in there for a bunch of assaults. I never asked him about that. Ratsy wasn't somebody you interrogated. Especially about personal stuff.

I never did figure out why Ratsy liked me, but for some reason he did. Which was good, because Ratsy was the toughest guy I've ever met. Tougher than Charlie Chen . . . tougher than Stink Pagler. But not just tough. Ratsy was dangerous. Scary dangerous. But he was never scary dangerous to me.

One time after gym he said to me, "It's a good thing I like you, Slater, because if I didn't I might have to kill you." Then he laughed for a long time. Hilarious.

There was a classroom in the Centre and we had to go to school every day. The teacher—I can't remember her name—was kind of a cool lady. She treated us like ordinary kids, and if she was afraid of anybody, even Ratsy, she never let on.

The first day she made us write an essay. We had to write about the first memory we had in our whole life. I had to think about it for a while. It's hard to remember stuff that happened so long ago, stuff you don't usually spend a lot of time thinking about. There were some things

I didn't want to write about, at least not for someone else to see. I ended up writing about a time when we'd gone camping at this lake. I was pretty little and it was the first time I'd ever been around water that wasn't in a bathtub or a puddle. My dad carried me the whole time we were in the water. Sometimes he'd lower me into the water, but as soon as I got scared he'd lift me out and carry me again. Having my dad looking after me like that was about the safest feeling there could be. I didn't write that part down.

When we finished, Ratsy and me traded and read each other's stories. I almost got sick reading what Ratsy had put down. He was a terrible writer. Most of the words were spelled wrong and a lot of the sentences didn't make sense. But that wasn't what made me sick. It was what he was writing about.

Eddie stopped writing. He wasn't sure he even wanted to *think* about the next part, let alone write it. He listened. No sounds but a few small animal noises.

"Hi guys," he said to the salamanders in the aquarium-looking cage directly across from him.

"I think I'm losing my damn mind." Eddie stretched his legs. "I'm talking to a bunch of animals, which is about the same as talking to myself. I'm going nuts."

He realized he hadn't thought about Ratsy for a long while. Funny how when somebody wasn't around, you stopped thinking about them after a while. He tucked his legs up under him again, looked at the floor and spoke slowly and softly.

"Ratsy's story was about this uncle who wasn't really an uncle at all but actually a friend of Ratsy's dad. This guy hung around their place a lot. One night Ratsy's dad and the uncle were doing some drugs, Ratsy didn't say what. After the two of them were pretty stoned the uncle decided maybe Ratsy should do some of the stuff, too. Ratsy didn't want to. He couldn't remember exactly how old he was, but he figured maybe seven or eight.

"Anyway, when Ratsy wouldn't do the drugs, the guy grabbed him by the hair and pushed his face down onto the lit burner of an electric stove. Ratsy's dad was either too stoned to notice or he didn't care. He didn't do anything except tell Ratsy to shut up when he screamed. As I was reading the story I looked over at Ratsy and noticed some marks on the side of his face. I'd seen them before but hadn't really thought about them until then. There wasn't much more to the story.

"As I was giving him back his story, I figured I should say something. 'Man, that must have hurt.'

"I can still remember Ratsy's answer almost word for word. 'Yeah, it was pretty bad, I guess, but the worst part was the smell of my face burning. Anyway, it didn't matter. There was lots worse stuff that happened to me after that.'"

Eddie stood up. His legs were stiff again from the cold and from sitting cross-legged. He thought maybe he'd write Ratsy's story into the notebook later. Right now it was time to get moving and to think about finding something to eat.

He stepped around the corner. Jack Simm wasn't there, but the paper bag he'd been carrying was on the floor. Eddie opened it. Inside was a sweater. It was one of the ugliest sweaters he'd ever seen. But it looked warm. Damn, did it look warm.

Six

He'd been dreaming. He'd been dreaming every night since the Stink Pagler thing. How long ago was that? Five, maybe six days. And how long since he'd gotten out of the house? It was getting hard to keep track. When you don't have a watch and there are no calendars, it's easy to lose your sense of time. Or at least of time passing. Last night's dream was pretty much the same as all the others. He didn't remember them exactly, except that there were faces that kept popping up in front of him. Sometimes it was Steve's and sometimes it was Stink Pagler's. Once it was Ratsy's face, but only the part that had been burned. All the faces seemed to be floating and there were no bodies. Every time Eddie woke up he was sweating, even though the nights were still cold. Then he'd lie there for a long time thinking about how dead he'd be if Stink Pagler ever found him. A few times he'd tried concentrating on Linda Chen's face as he was falling asleep in the hope that maybe he'd dream about her instead. It hadn't worked.

He was glad now that he hadn't told Linda where he was hanging out. Not that she would tell if she could help it. But you could never be sure with somebody like Stink.

The day was a slow one around the zoo. Eddie had decided a few days earlier that, since he was there anyway, he was going to become an expert on everything that lived there. Or at least the animals that really interested him. He figured this would be a good day to start. First he got himself a coffee—actually, two cups. It was a trick he'd used lots of times before. You bought the coffee, hustled around the corner of the building and grabbed an empty cup off the ground or out of a garbage can. A quick rinse under the water fountain and then back to the concession stand looking sad. The key was to find a friendly clerk and look pathetic while relating the tragic tale of how you'd spilled the coffee before you had even one drink. Eddie was pretty good at this kind of story. Today he threw in a few details—it was a rude, fat man who had jostled him and made him spill the coffee.

The play almost always worked. He took his two cups of coffee and headed off to the Large Mammal Building to spend a couple of hours studying a family of gorillas. He realized fairly quickly that he hadn't made the best choice. There were a number of things about gorillas that reminded him of Stink Pagler.

Studying the gorillas was a lot better than biology class. For one thing he wasn't sitting in a desk. He hated that part of school. There had been some kind of study one time about learning styles. Eddie had actually read the results. It said that people learn in different ways. He couldn't remember all the proper terms, but he did remember that some people have to move around more when they learn. Eddie figured whoever did the study must have been pretty smart. There'd been times when he thought he'd bust if he had to sit in his desk for one more minute. But there were always lots more minutes. At the zoo he could move anytime he wanted.

The Large Mammal Building was excellent. Eddie figured that if you couldn't be out in the wild, this wouldn't be so bad. He decided he liked being near the gorillas after all. There was a sign on the outside of the enclosure telling people that gorillas preferred visitors to stay back from the glass and not smack it with their hands to get the animals' attention.

Eddie remembered something from one of those Discovery Channel documentaries. If you stayed low, so that the gorilla was on your level or higher, and didn't stare right at them but rather glanced then looked away, the animals would sometimes come close to check you out. He was about to try out this theory when a guy and his girlfriend came into the building.

Eddie had already concluded that at least half of the people who came here paid no attention to the sign's request. They stuck their faces against the glass, made stupid noises, stared and even laughed at the gorillas. This guy was even stupider than most. He was late twenties, maybe thirty. He jumped around and scratched his armpits. His girlfriend laughed like the guy was Jerry Seinfeld. Eddie was glad when they left. He wasn't sure, but it seemed like the gorillas were insulted. They had turned their backs to the glass when the man was doing his routine and they stayed that way for a long time after the couple left. They didn't move. They just sat staring at the back part of the enclosure.

Eddie was alone in the building after the couple left. He sat across from the gorillas, watching and writing little notes in the notebook. Finally, after several minutes, one of the animals turned and looked at Eddie.

"Don't worry, not all of us are that stupid," Eddie said quietly. Then he slowly crept toward the enclosure, careful not to stare.

The gorilla, a huge female, came toward the glass and stood motionless. It was as if she was studying him. Moving slowly, Eddie set the notebook down on the floor and edged closer to the glass. He stopped, and for what seemed like a very long time Eddie and the gorilla stood close to each other, separated only by the glass. Still, Eddie didn't look directly at her.

The gorilla slowly raised one arm and pressed a leathery hand against the glass. After a few seconds Eddie raised his own hand and put it on the glass right opposite the gorilla's. Eddie wondered if it meant something—he wanted to believe it did, sort of like the gorilla was saying, *I like you better than Mr. Armpits*—but there was no way of knowing for sure.

After a couple of minutes, Eddie heard the sound of people coming into the building. The gorilla must have heard it too because she took her hand down and backed away from the window. Whatever the moment between them had meant, it was over.

By noon Eddie was hungry, but he decided to wait a while before getting something to eat. His money was running out. Since he was in no hurry to start doing B and E's again, he had decided to cut down to eating only twice a day, and maybe only once if he could stand it.

He left the Large Mammal Building and walked around for a while. Finally he sat down on a bench next to one of the old-style animal cages. It wasn't used anymore. It was just a display to show how much things had improved for animals in zoos. After a while Eddie got up and went inside the cage to see what it must have been like to live in there. He didn't like it much. He paced around, pretending he was a lion or something. He even roared a few times for effect. Then he remembered the guy at the gorilla enclosure and decided not to do any more animal impersonations. As he stepped out of the cage, Eddie decided that living in there would be right up there with spending time at the Calgary Young Offenders Centre.

He went back and sat on the bench outside the cage. He'd picked that bench in the first place because a terrific-looking woman was eating an ice-cream cone not far away. He'd been watching her for a while. Eddie didn't think she'd noticed him at all, not even when he was pacing around the cage and roaring.

He liked watching great-looking women. Sometimes he imagined himself married to someone like that and taking her to nice restaurants and plays and stuff at the Jubilee Auditorium. At least this lady didn't look like she was a Schwarzenegger fan. He was tempted to go over and ask her what she thought of *You've Got Mail*. He didn't get the chance. A kid, maybe four or five years old, came around the corner and ran up to the woman. The kid was also working on an ice-cream cone. Eddie lost interest.

He'd just noticed that one of his pant legs was beginning to fray at the bottom, when someone sat down next to him. Eddie didn't even have to look up. He knew who it was.

"You want a *whole* Coke?" Jack Simm asked.

The question meant that Jack had been watching him for a while. A few minutes earlier he had taken half a cup of Coke that a woman—not the one with the kid—left on a picnic table. The cup was empty now, but he was still holding it when Jack sat down. Eddie still wasn't sure about Jack Simm. He'd been around long enough to know that if you wanted to stay healthy you didn't get into conversations with nut jobs. And it just made sense that anyone following a lone teenage kid around a zoo could be a nut job. Nut job as in pervert.

"No thanks." Eddie didn't want to be indebted any more than necessary. That's when he realized he was wearing the sweater Jack had left in the Reptile Building. He wished he hadn't worn the sweater today.

"Suit yourself," Jack answered. "I'm getting myself one and then I'm coming back here to sit. So, you writing a book or something?"

Eddie decided not to answer. It wasn't any of the old man's business. "Look, thanks for the sweater, but I'd really like it if you didn't follow me around anymore."

"I'm going up there to get myself a hot dog and a Coke. Then I'm coming back here to sit down." Jack got up and went to the concession stand. He didn't look at Eddie on his way there or on his way back. It was like he knew Eddie would still be there. Or maybe he just didn't give a damn. Except when he got back to the bench he was carrying two hot dogs and two Cokes. He set one of the Cokes and one of the hot dogs on the bench between them.

They sat there, not saying anything. Jack was eating slowly and looking off at the grey-blue sky. Eddie considered leaving, but he didn't want the old man to think he could just come by and take over the bench. Eddie had been there first. He didn't touch the Coke or the hot dog, although he was getting hungrier and the hot dog smelled good.

"Last Sam's cage," Jack said.

Eddie turned his head toward him but kept his eyes looking away. "What?"

The man pointed over his shoulder with his thumb. "That cage. Last Sam lived in there. Black bear. Lived in there six, maybe seven years. He was the last animal to live in that kind of cage. Sam wasn't his real name. It was the name I gave him. I called every bear that lived in that cage Sam. Don't know why. Guess I just thought the name fit. And since he was the last Sam to live there, that makes this Last Sam's cage."

Jack took a bite of his hot dog. Eddie thought about being rude and telling him that he couldn't care less about the damn bear or the hot dog. He decided against the idea, although he wasn't sure why. He went back to studying the cuff on his pants.

"I don't blame you for not trusting a guy who hangs around the zoo. But that's no reason not to eat the food."

Eddie picked up the Coke and sipped it. He left the hot dog where it was sitting. "Yeah, well . . . thanks . . . for the hot dog." He finally looked at Jack, but the old man seemed interested only in the wrapper around his hot dog.

Jack stuck out his hand. "You're welcome, kid."

Eddie shook the hand. It felt okay, not a wimp shake or a cop shake or anything. He didn't say his name. "You really come here every day?"

Jack Simm nodded and bit into his hot dog again.

"Why?"

"Thirty-two years. Every day. I've been coming so long they let me in for free." Jack Simm nodded. "It's sort of like they gave me a lifetime pass."

The old man hadn't answered his question. Eddie decided to try again. "You must really like animals."

"They're all right. Sometimes I think it would be better if the animals were running free and the people were locked up in zoos."

That was weird. It was almost word for word the thought Eddie had had when he'd been watching the guy at the gorilla enclosure. Eddie didn't know how to answer so he didn't say anything.

"It isn't the animals I come for." Jack looked over at him. "I like them, but it's not what brings me here any more than it's what brought you here."

Eddie wasn't sure what he should say to that either. He reached down and picked up the hot dog. "You sure you don't want this?"

Jack just shrugged. Eddie took a bite, then another. Even though Jack had a head start, Eddie finished his hot dog first.

"I figured you might be hungry," Jack said.

"You must think you know a lot."

"Not so much, really, but I know just about everything there is to know about this place, and I know there's a runaway kid hiding out here. You ever hear what happened to your friend Ratsy?"

So you stayed and listened after all, Eddie thought. He wasn't sure if he was happy about that or not.

"Yeah," Eddie said slowly. "I heard something about him a few weeks after I got out. Ratsy and another guy were doing a B and E at some house. The old man who lived in the place got up to go to the bathroom and stumbled right into them. One of them, I never heard which, hit the old man with a two-by-four or something like that and now he's in a coma. I heard it didn't look like he was going to get better. He'd just stay in the coma and eventually die.

"They were trying to get Ratsy into adult court on the deal. I don't imagine Ratsy gave a damn one way or the other. He probably didn't give a damn about the old man either. Ratsy was the only person I ever knew who really didn't care if he lived or died."

Jack shook his head but didn't say anything. He put the last of his hot dog in his mouth, then stood up and walked to a garbage container a few feet away. He dropped the wrapper and his napkin carefully into the container.

Without turning back, he said, "Look after yourself, kid." He said it so low, Eddie barely heard him. It was all Jack said. Then he walked off in the direction of the polar bear enclosure.

Eddie sat for a long time, drinking the rest of his Coke and thinking. Jack Simm had come to the zoo every day for thirty-two years. Why would anybody do that? Weird guy. Not wacko weird like Stink Pagler but weird just the same.

Seven

Eddie had begun to wonder how much longer he could hold out. It had rained most of the night, the third night in a row. No rain had actually found its way into the shed, but the place was even colder and clammier than usual. He was afraid if it didn't warm up soon, he'd freeze to death. It might be months before they found his body, still frozen solid in a curled-up ball on a piece of cardboard advertising Xerox photocopiers.

He could hear noises in the night, too. They seemed to be all around him. Eddie liked animals, but he preferred them to be on the other side of something, a wall or glass—something. These noises were a little too close. If sleeping in the storage shed meant sharing space with mice and bugs, someone was going to have to leave. He figured the smaller creatures could have the place—just as soon as he could find somewhere else to sleep.

The rain quit by morning and the heavy low clouds finally gave way to blue sky. The early sunshine felt good. For the first time in days, Eddie began to feel warm. The morning started off well. For one thing he had a decent breakfast consisting of french fries—he bought those—a perfectly good apple someone had left on the ground beside a picnic table and more than half a cup of luke-warm coffee. He'd ripped off the coffee from a woman who had left it on the table while she took her daughter to the bathroom in the plant conservatory.

When he finished eating, Eddie took what was left of the coffee and stretched out on the grass on the side of a little hill. Despite all the rain the grass here was dry. He had to make some decisions and he had to make them soon. Money was becoming a problem. He was almost broke and even with careful managing of what money he had left, he'd be out soon. It was almost time to think about a B and E. But not quite yet. He'd only left the zoo once in his three weeks of living here and wasn't really looking forward to leaving again. The Stink Pagler encounter had scared him. Scared him a lot.

He was stretched out with his arm under his head as a pillow. It felt good to be warm and he was almost asleep. He didn't hear or see Jack Simm approach.

"Doesn't look to me like you did a lot of planning before you ran away," Jack said, then threw a sleeping bag down beside Eddie. "Maybe you can use this."

Eddie sat up. "Yeah . . . I mean, yeah, I can use it. Thanks. But don't you—"

"You know the little stream on the other side of Dinny?" Jack interrupted.

Eddie looked over in the direction of Dinny—the huge life-size model of a brontosaurus that had acted as the zoo's unofficial symbol for more than forty years. The first time Eddie had seen Dinny he'd calculated that a

76

pickup truck could pass under the dinosaur's belly without touching.

"Yeah, I know it."

"Along the west bank, about halfway down between Dinny and the walking bridge that goes over the stream, there are a couple of good places to sleep. Dry, out of the wind and hidden so nobody will see you unless you get careless. Better than where you're sleeping now. Take a look."

That was it. Jack Simm had said what he'd come to say and he walked off. It was almost as if he'd read Eddie's mind. Eddie wondered if he should tell him thanks for the advice but that he was fine where he was. But inside, he already knew that as soon as it was safe he'd check out the place Jack had told him about. Eddie watched the strange man go and then moved the sleeping bag so he could rest his head on it. He fell asleep almost instantly.

After the zoo had closed, Eddie headed for the man-made stream that ran north and south just on the other side of Dinny. He took his time, making sure that no one was in the area before hopping the waist-high chain-link fence that bordered the stream. He was glad the fence was there. It would discourage people from trying to get close to the stream bank to get a better look at the birds that resided there. They were mostly ducks and geese, although some were pretty exotic-looking.

He dropped down on the other side of the fence and tried to blend in with the shrubs and small trees that grew along the banks. The birds didn't seem to appreciate the visit. Eddie moved as slowly and quietly as he could to keep them from getting too upset. A bunch of frantic bird noise might bring one of the zookeepers or a security type to see what was going on.

It wasn't long before the ducks and geese calmed down. They'd probably seen a lot more people than birds in the wild do. After a few minutes they didn't pay any attention to him at all.

Eddie looked around and smiled. Jack Simm had been right. In fact, the place was even better than Eddie had imagined. With the trees and shrubs that grew on both sides of the stream, people walking by just a few feet away wouldn't be able to see him. And it would be even better in the summer when the trees leafed out. But the best part was the bed. He found it right away. It wasn't really a bed, but after the storage shed, it might as well have been. About midway between where he had hopped the fence and the little bridge was a ledge that jutted out a couple of feet over the water. Underneath the ledge, the bank cut away into a little opening about as wide as two of Eddie and a little longer than his height. It was perfect.

As soon as he saw it he knew this had to be the place Jack had talked about. He'd be sheltered from the wind and the rain and—most of all—from people. The only tricky part was getting in and out of the little space. He had to slither in from one end, feet first. He took a look around to make sure no one was watching and got down on the ground to work his way inside. It wasn't easy, but he thought he'd get better with practice.

As great as it looked from the outside, it was even better inside. The floor of the space was soft, mostly moss and old pine needles. When Eddie was inside and stretched out, it reminded him of camping except this was better than a tent. A lot better.

Things had definitely improved. Two weeks earlier he'd almost had a fatal encounter with Stink Pagler. Now, here he was relaxing in about the best place he could ever remember being. Lying there, Eddie felt happier than he'd been since Steve moved in with his mother.

Of course, there was still Jack Simm. What if he *was* a pervert? What if this was a setup for him to be able to get at Eddie? Now the old man would know exactly where he was. Eddie thought about it, but not for long. In the first place, Jack had obviously known about the storage shed. He hadn't come around—or at least if he had, Eddie hadn't seen him. And besides, the little space was too small for anyone much bigger than himself. But that wasn't the only thing. Jack was different, no doubt about that. Maybe he even had some mental problem, which would at least explain his coming to the zoo every day for thirty-two years. But there was something that made Eddie think Jack wasn't a kid molester. In fact, he was sure of it. Pretty sure. But just in case he was wrong, he dug out his Swiss Army knife and stuck it into the ground near his head with the blade open. He'd keep it there whenever he was in the little cave.

The water of the stream lapped right up to the edge of his bed. It would be cool to wake up in the morning and see a twig or leaf floating right by his face. Eddie had never liked to go to bed at night. When he was little, it was always a battle with his mom and dad. As he got older, he liked to stay up late and watch movies or listen to music. Or hang out with his friends somewhere. Somewhere far from his house.

But tonight he couldn't wait to get to bed. First he'd have to make one last trip to the storage shed. He had to gather up his clothes and find a place close to the new sleeping space to stash them. He'd have to be extra careful. Now that life was starting to look brighter, this was no time to get found out.

It was more than an hour before he had his clothes safely stashed under a smaller ledge just a few steps from his new bed. He manoeuvred the sleeping bag Jack had given him down onto the soft floor of the opening. Then he worked his way into the space and spent a long time adjusting the sleeping bag, and himself, this way and that until everything felt just right.

At last he was comfortable. But he didn't go to sleep right away. There was a lot to think about. What should he call this place? It wasn't really a cave, but he wanted to give it a name. He'd have to think about that.

He listened to the sounds. They were good sounds, safe ones. The ducks and geese were making little night noises and he could hear the water gurgling softly right next to him. Once he was sure he heard some animal walk over the ledge right above. He couldn't tell what it was, probably something small. That made him think about what could happen if one of the zookeepers forgot to lock an enclosure, like, say, the lion's.

Eddie had quite a few weird thoughts that night. He thought about Ratsy and wondered where he was. Probably in jail somewhere. Eddie fell asleep wishing Ratsy could see the place he was in at that moment.

Eight

He was wrong. The first thing he saw when he woke up wasn't a twig or a leaf. It was a duck, quite small and all brown and curious. Eddie remembered from biology that the duller-coloured birds were females. Her bill was practically against his face and he could see her feet moving in the water beneath her. They looked at each other for a while. Then the duck gave a little quack and swam off.

After that he saw a lot of her. In fact, it became a kind of ritual. Every morning when he opened his eyes, the duck was there like a feathery alarm clock. He was positive it was the same duck because she never missed a day. He had no way of knowing how long she was there before he opened his eyes. But each time she was in almost the same spot, sometimes looking at him, other times ignoring him completely, and eventually swimming off to do whatever ducks did with their day.

Eddie liked to read. He couldn't remember a time when he didn't like reading. He could remember his dad reading out loud when he was little. When he got older they switched roles and Eddie did the reading. If his dad ever got tired of all those Kjelgaard stories Eddie was into back then, he never let on. Eddie read *Big Red* out loud so many times he could still remember a lot of it, even after all this time. He'd always liked Saturdays at home because Steve usually left the house early and Eddie could stay in bed with a book until his mother decided it was time he got up and had breakfast. Sometimes he'd knock off a whole book in a morning, especially something easy like the Hardy Boys or some other mystery. He didn't read the Hardy Boys or Kjelgaard anymore, but he still liked mysteries. It was funny, but when he was reading he didn't mind being still. Maybe that whole learning-style thing didn't apply to reading.

It was kind of embarrassing being a reader. None of the guys he hung out with would be caught dead reading a book and he had to put up with lots of comments. Sometimes the comments weren't all that funny. Probably because they weren't meant to be.

Just now, Jack London was the number-one author on Eddie's list. He'd written a book report on *The Call of the Wild* for Miss Shackleton and had got an A on it. And now he was rereading *White Fang*. He'd always wanted a dog of his own, but his dad had said the yard in Long Prairie was too small for a dog. And they'd always rented after they moved to the city. Rental places never allowed dogs. Maybe that was the best part of living at the zoo. It was like having a few hundred animals for pets. And he didn't even have to feed them.

Reading in the "condo"—that's what he'd decided to call the place—was one of those good news/bad news deals. Eddie soon learned that he could lie there as long as he wanted and even in a driving rain—there had been a fair amount already that spring—not a drop of water found its way in. That was good. The bad part was that even on bright sunny days, the condo remained quite dark. And once the sun went down, reading time was over. He needed a flashlight.

In fact, more than food or money, the thing that drove him most toward attempting a B and E was the need for a light to read by. Actually, there were a few things he needed—like a Walkman. He wished he could listen to music once in a while. That was something else he hoped to grab. And, of course, a little money wouldn't hurt either.

Since he couldn't read after dark, nights were the worst times. Boredom was the part of his new life that he hated the most. He had thought a few times about going to see Charlie and maybe Linda in Chinatown. But something kept him from going. Fear? Eddie had never been a coward. But the longer he was free, the more he wanted to stay that way. And his luck with cops had never been great. So why push it? Charlie—and Linda—would have to wait.

Nighttime was also when he did most of his thinking. That was bad because thinking about things at night made them seem worse than when he thought about them during the day. Sometimes he worried about what would happen to him. He tried not to spend a lot of time on that, but it was impossible not to. Spring was about to roll into summer, but even summer would eventually end. He knew that if he didn't have a real home or job by then he'd have to become a lot more active on the crime scene. And he wasn't sure that was what he wanted. It was more than the dread of getting caught again, although there was nothing he hated more than the thought of being back in the CYOC. But this was a different feeling. Eddie had started to wonder if maybe there wasn't something else, something better. One thing was for sure. He didn't want to end up like the Stink Paglers of the world. Or even the Ratsys.

That was something else he thought about when darkness surrounded the stream and the condo: there was one very badass creep out there who wasn't about to forget what Eddie had done. And if they ever met again—even if it was five years later—Eddie didn't like the idea of how it might turn out.

May 26, 4:15 P.M. (I checked out the date and time by looking through an office window. Calendar and clock side by side on one of the walls. Bingo.)

Okay, time for a little self-humiliation. I'm going to write about my first bath since I ran away. I mean, it's not like I haven't been washing—I give myself a good scrub in one of the bathrooms pretty well every day. You never know when a babefest might break out around here and I want to be ready. The weather's been the pits again. In fact, it's been so bad for so many days that I haven't even spent much time wandering around. I've mostly been hanging out inside buildings.

But the sun finally came out a couple of days ago and started drying the mud that was everywhere. And today is the warmest yet. I decided to celebrate the arrival of a real summer-type day by having a bath. That doesn't happen to be as easy as it sounds. I woke up early and after my morning duck swam off, I stripped naked inside the condo (which took a lot of wiggling around and a fairly long time) and then I just rolled out into the water.

It was like ice. Worse than ice. I was even colder than some of those nights I spent in the storage shed. I didn't do much splashing, I was too cold. I couldn't use soap in the creek—that would've been bad for the birds—so I rubbed water all over myself—rubbed so hard it hurt—and got out of there in a hurry.

I'll tell you one thing: as I was standing there naked and shivering and trying to dry myself off with a T-shirt (I forgot to bring towels), I was thinking it might be a long time before I had another creek bath. Babefest or no babefest.

I also worked out a way to wash my hair. A few days ago I found a plastic pail left behind by a workman or someone on the zoo staff. I left it out in the rain for a few days. Don't they always tell you that rainwater is good for the scalp? Anyway, after I stopped shivering from the bath, I got the pail of water and a plastic bottle of shampoo (finally something I actually remembered to bring from home), then I walked off a little way from the creek and gave myself a very natural hair wash. Natural but not convenient. Or fun. I don't think I ever fully appreciated just how useful a bathtub is.

I have to admit this is the cleanest I've felt in a long time. I was feeling pretty good, too, so I decided to take a long walk around the zoo. It was good to see the animals out of their houses for a change. They probably felt the same way I did. I got out my notebook and spent a long time watching the polar bears. I like polar bears. In fact, I think it would be cool being one. Not only do you get to live in the North where there aren't a lot of people to bug you, but when you're that big and tough you aren't going to get hassled much, even if somebody does come around.

Eddie had eaten lunch while watching the polar bears—mostly scrounged stuff people had left uneaten and a ripped-off bag of chips. Then he resumed his stroll. As he was passing the children's playground that occupied an area not far from the main concession stand, he saw Jack Simm sitting on the ground. With all the crappy weather, he hadn't seen Jack for a while. Eddie decided this was as good a time as any to thank him for the sleeping bag and the tip on the place to sleep.

Jack was sitting with his knees up and his arms crossed over them. Eddie sat down next to him. Jack wasn't wearing a coat, just a sweatshirt with University of Saskatchewan written across the front and what looked like the same pants he'd been wearing the other times Eddie had seen him.

Eddie looked at Jack Simm. There was something strange about the way the man was watching the kids in that playground. He was staring at them, concentrating like he was studying them or something. Eddie didn't like it. Here was a guy who sat and looked at little kids playing on swings and slides and who also knew where Eddie slept. That wasn't good at all. Eddie didn't say anything to Jack, not even about the sleeping bag. He just sat and watched the man watching the kids. Jack never looked at him or said a word; it was like he didn't even know Eddie was there.

They sat like that for a long time. It got later and finally the last mother and child left the playground and headed for the parking lot.

"How's your day been?" Jack spoke suddenly without turning to look at him.

"Okay, I guess, how about yours?"

Jack nodded for an answer. Eddie thought he might say something about hanging out at the playground, but he didn't.

"Feel like a coffee?" Jack got up and brushed grass off his pants.

Eddie stood up, too. "I'll buy." They walked to the concession stand and Eddie bought two cups of coffee. Jack didn't argue about it. Eddie liked that. A lot of adults figured they were supposed to pay for everything when they were with kids. Eddie had always thought that was crap, a way to remind kids that they weren't important enough to do adult stuff like pay for things.

They sat on a bench by the conservatory and drank the coffee. When he'd finished, Jack got up, nodded and walked off. Eddie watched him go. The man sure wasn't a big talker. Eddie sat a while longer, thinking about Jack Simm. He didn't know why a grown man would sit at a playground and watch kids the way Jack had been doing. It was strange—there was no doubt about that. But he still didn't want to believe it was because Jack got his jollies from kids.

Trouble was, he'd been wrong about people before. When Steve first moved in with his mom, Eddie had figured he was sort of cool. The three of them had done some stuff together—movies and stuff—and things were okay until that time Steve had gone after Eddie's mother. Eddie had been big-time wrong about Steve. He hoped he wasn't wrong now.

Nine

It was curiosity. That's what Eddie decided when he thought about why he'd followed Jack Simm home a few days after their conversation. He wanted to know more about the man who came to the zoo almost every day of his life and then spent his time sitting around watching kids at a playground. What kind of person did that? Where did he live? What did he do with the rest of his time?

Eddie could have asked Jack Simm some of those questions, and maybe he would one day. But as far as where he lived—what kind of place it was—he could find that out just by following the man home. Eddie was good at following people. It was something he'd practiced back when he read all those Hardy Boys books and wanted to be a detective.

Jack was easy to follow. He didn't look back once. In fact, he hardly even looked up; mostly, he just stared at the ground as he walked, like he was thinking hard about things. For a man who almost magically seemed to know all about Eddie's life at the zoo, he didn't appear to be particularly observant.

They left the zoo over the swinging footbridge that led north, Eddie staying far enough back to avoid being recognized if Jack did turn around. It was only the second time in all the weeks he'd been at the zoo that Eddie had left the place, and it felt good to be out and travelling around again.

They crossed the busy freeway that bordered that perimeter of the zoo, then continued north. Eddie was glad Jack didn't look back because for a while there were no houses or buildings to duck behind. Eventually they came to an older residential neighbourhood. Eddie recognized it as Bridgeland—his aunt lived around here somewhere, although Eddie wasn't sure he could find the place on foot. He'd always gone there in a car.

He passed what looked like a nursing home on his left, with the rubble of what had once been the General Hospital behind it. Eddie remembered reading that a lot of people had been pissed off about the hospital being closed and eventually demolished as part of government cutbacks. Eddie didn't know much about politics, but the great gash in the landscape where there had once been a hospital was depressing.

On his right was a school for the mentally handicapped. Just past the school Jack Simm turned right, went slightly uphill for a block and turned left. Eddie hung back, then moved ahead slowly and carefully. When he reached the corner where Jack had made his second turn, Eddie didn't see anyone. For a minute he thought he'd lost the man and he cursed under his breath. Then he heard a door close and spotted someone disappearing into a house on the left side of the street. He couldn't tell if it was Jack Simm or not.

Eddie waited a few minutes, then crossed the street in order to stay behind the parked cars lining that side of the road. He stopped when he was directly across from the house he'd seen the person go into. He made a mental note of the number—one-eleven. As he looked at the house he was sure that this was where Jack Simm lived. The house was small and there were bushes everywhere in the front yard. One tall spruce tree stood on either side of the sidewalk that led up to the door. It was the kind of house that would be a piece of cake to break into: lots of cover, the front door in shadow from the trees. Eddie figured he could get in and out of the place in broad daylight without anybody knowing.

But would he? It wasn't that he wanted to steal anything from Jack, especially after the man had been pretty decent to him so far. But maybe there was something in the house that might offer a clue as to why the guy behaved the way he did. And besides, it was reasonable, wasn't it? If Jack Simm was a pervert, Eddie had a right to know. No, he *needed* to know. For his own safety.

He made up his mind. He'd do it tomorrow. No sense putting it off. While Jack Simm was sitting watching the kids at the playground, Eddie would see if he could find out more about the mystery man.

He didn't get to put his plan into effect, at least not right away. The next day the weather turned bad again. This time there was snow mixed in with the rain that fell for most of the day. There was one good thing that happened though. Someone left a ski jacket lying on a table in the conservatory, probably while they went to the bathroom. Eddie looked quickly around, picked up the jacket and hurried out of the building. He went straight back to the condo and stashed the jacket. He wouldn't be able to wear it at least for a few days. The person who owned it—*used to own it*, Eddie smiled—would probably report it missing and the security people would be on the lookout. He felt a little guilty about ruining the jacket owner's day, but he told himself that anybody who could afford a jacket like that could probably afford two.

The ugly weather lasted only that day. The next morning was one of the warmest so far and Eddie decided it was an ideal time to check out Jack's place. He took no chances, waiting until he spotted the old man sitting near the kids' playground before he left the zoo. He made a last stop at the concession stand with the hope of finding something decent left uneaten or at least untended, something he could take with him for the walk to Jack's house. This time he was unsuccessful. He'd have to make the walk to Bridgeland without a snack.

It wasn't a long walk—maybe twenty minutes if you went straight at it—but Eddie deliberately took a roundabout route. Might as well kill two birds with one stone, he thought as he checked out potential B and E locations in the blocks around Jack's place. He settled on an infill-type house as a good candidate, particularly after he saw a woman leaving with a briefcase in hand. The woman drove off in a newer Jeep Grand Cherokee. Leather seats. *Yes!* Eddie liked the set-up. The almost-new house and the yuppie vehicle indicated money, and the fact that the woman carried a briefcase in hand suggested the house was likely to be vacant during the day. It wasn't a perfect target—there were no mature trees or bushes in the yard and the house was on a narrow lot that put it almost up against its neighbours. But you couldn't have everything. Besides, he'd check the place out at least one more time before he made his move.

As he got closer to Jack's, Eddie slowed his pace in order to get a good look at the houses on either side of one-eleven and across the street. He walked to the end of the block and turned the corner, never looking back. He'd learned long before that looking straight ahead and from side to side was okay, but looking back tended to draw attention. You looked nervous, which was never a good idea.

When he reached the back lane that ran behind Jack's house, he turned again, now focusing his attention on the houses on the opposite side of the alley. There was no one outside cutting the lawn or hanging wash and Eddie couldn't see anybody looking out a window. All seemed quiet. Time to make his move. He hopped the low wire fence that ran along the rear of Jack's property and headed quickly for the back door. He tried to turn the handle—once in a while you got lucky—but it was locked.

Eddie faded into the shadows created by a stand of over-grown bushes at the corner of the house. He thought about the front door, recalling that it offered good cover, but he didn't like the idea that it faced the street. There were two windows in this part of the back wall. One was a main-floor window. It sat directly over a smaller window that obviously led to the basement. Eddie chose the lower one. People tended to pay less attention to the security of their basement windows.

Jack Simm was one of those people. The window was locked, but a pane of glass had been broken some time before and replaced with a piece of plywood. Whatever was holding the plywood in place—if anything was—wasn't very effective. Eddie took a glove out of his pocket. It was a glove he'd made for himself after some advice from Ratsy. The palm was covered with an adhesive substance. You didn't want to push a pane of glass, or in this case, wood, into the house where they would fall to the floor and make noise. Instead, you cut or broke them and drew them out with the sticky glove.

This time no cutting or breaking was needed. Eddie placed the glove against the plywood and pulled it out easily, so easily he was forced to smile. Either Jack Simm was a very trusting man or he didn't have anything in the house worth stealing.

Eddie reached inside the vacant window frame and quickly undid the fastener. One more swift look around and Eddie began his feet-first slide into the house and down onto the basement floor. Another small smile as he thought about how getting in and out of his condo was good practice for what he was doing now. As his feet hit the floor he dropped quickly into a crouch, looking and listening hard for anything that might provide a warning, an indication that something was wrong. Nothing. No movement, no sound, save a quiet hum to his left—the pilot light of the furnace—and the staccato sound of his own breathing, short, quick breaths more from nervousness than exertion. This was always the scariest part—the first few seconds in the house. What if Jack Simm lived with someone else and that person was in the house now?

Still no noise, at least none that needed to be feared. Eddie moved slowly toward the stairs, stopping after a few steps to listen again. Now he was certain there was no one here, no one but him. The basement didn't have much in it: a few cardboard boxes, a red metal tool box, a pile of old magazines and a broken wooden chair. Nothing to tell Eddie much about the man who lived here. It was funny that he felt so apprehensive about this particular break-in. Was it because he'd never broken into the house of anyone he knew before? Even though he wasn't planning to steal anything, there was something about what he was doing that felt more wrong than when it was done to strangers.

He started up the stairs to the main floor. A couple of the steps creaked and he stopped after each unwelcome sound. He wasn't fearful now, just cautious. There was no need for fear. He'd done this enough to know the danger signs and to know when things were okay. They were okay this time.

At the top of the stairs Eddie stopped and looked around the corner into the kitchen. Satisfied, he ducked low to avoid being seen through the window and started across the floor. He stopped in the middle of the tiny room and glanced around. It was fairly neat, cupboards along one wall, sink below the window. There was no room for a table. Several bananas sat, yellow and inviting, on the counter next to the sink. Eddie couldn't remember the last time he'd eaten a banana. There were six. Did people keep track of something like bananas? He decided they didn't and broke his vow not to take anything from Jack's house. He tore one banana from the bunch and stuffed it into his pocket.

Still staying low, he made his way to the living room and again peeked around the corner before moving farther. His eyes scanned the room with practiced precision, taking it in quickly and thoroughly. The curtains that covered the room's lone window were closed. They were heavy with a print pattern of flowers and windmills that Eddie was sure had been out of style for a long time. No one would see him through these curtains. He'd be able to move around without having to crouch. He eased his way around the corner, straightened up and looked around again, this time for detail. He was standing next to a chesterfield, old like the curtains. There was a small black-and-white television perched on a TV tray and sitting against the front door. Eddie was glad he'd decided to come in through the basement window.

The room was spare and dull. There were no pictures on the walls, no bookcases, none of the little knick-knacks people normally had on shelves. In fact, there weren't any shelves. A second TV tray was folded up against the far end of the couch. A big closet-looking cupboard stood in one corner, bringing to a total of three the pieces of furniture in the room, not counting the TV trays. No wonder the man spent all his time at the zoo. This had to be the most boring house on the planet.

There was one thing that seemed completely out of place. A glass-topped, wooden case sat on the floor, almost out of sight behind the couch. Eddie crossed the room and bent down for a look. Inside were rows of knives—four rows, five knives in each row. They came in different shapes and sizes. The smaller knives, some no bigger than a jackknife, were along the top of the case. Below them were larger ones, including one that stretched from one end of the case to the other. No two knives had the same handle. But they all had one thing in common: all of them looked expensive and each was polished so well that it shone, even in the room's dim light.

"Damn," Eddie whispered to himself. "I could live for six months on the money I'd get from one of those." But something stopped him from opening the glass and picking up one of the knives. Something told him that these meant more to Jack than anything else he owned, which wasn't saying much given the quality of the stuff in the room. Still, the knives seemed personal somehow and Eddie didn't feel comfortable even being this close to them. He straightened up.

There was another doorway leading to a room off to the right. Eddie almost decided not to bother with it but changed his mind. He'd come all this way and so far had learned almost nothing about the man who seemed to know so much about him. Might as well see it all. The room was obviously the bedroom and if Jack Simm was some kind of pervert, it made sense that the bedroom might offer up the evidence.

Eddie crossed the living room and looked through the doorway. The room was dark, with no window to offer any outside light. The light from the living room allowed him to get a general idea of the layout. The room was small, not much more than a glorified closet; in fact, Eddie was pretty sure it had probably *been* a closet at one time. A narrow bed, neatly made, took up most of what space there was. At the foot of the bed was a desk with a wooden chair, the kind that folds up, shoved partway into the opening under the surface. There was a lamp and other stuff, too, but Eddie couldn't make it out in the dark. He crossed to the lamp. He could risk turning it on in here. There was no chance anyone outside would see the light.

He turned on the light and stepped back, slowly taking in a breath then holding it for a long time. He suddenly wished he hadn't come at all. He was right to have been suspicious of Jack Simm. The walls were covered with pictures of children—little girls. The biggest concentration was directly over the desk, and there were more pictures on the desk itself. Some were snapshots, all of them black and white. But just as many were clippings from newspapers. Old newspapers with paper the yellow of dying grass.

Eddie leaned forward and studied the pictures. The girls were young, much younger than Eddie. They had to be six, maybe seven years old. The pictures weren't pornographic, in fact most of them looked like family photos. Maybe Jack had stolen them. But why would somebody do that? And why were all the pictures so old?

And then it was clear. It was the newspaper clippings that told him. And as he read, Eddie felt the same way he had when he'd read Ratsy's essay in the Young Offenders Centre. He thought he might throw up. He took deep breaths and willed himself not to. It helped that there was nothing in his stomach to get rid of. But repulsed as he was by the story that was so carefully laid out in front of him, Eddie couldn't pull himself away. He had to read it all. He had to know it all. He slowly eased himself into the folding chair.

The pictures weren't of different girls. They were all of the same girl. Some included other people, but most were of her alone. Many were repeats of other pictures, sometimes larger or smaller. Eddie looked at the wall over the bed. It looked like some of his friends' bedroom walls, especially the guys', with dozens of pictures of a favourite athlete or rock singer.

Except the little girl in these pictures wasn't an athlete or rock singer. The torn newspaper clipping taped on the wall directly in front of Eddie told the story. The headline was in huge bold letters: "CHILD SLAIN".

Eddie looked again and again at the largest picture of the girl. It was right below the headline. She was happy, smiling for the camera; maybe a parent or teacher had snapped the photo. The details of the girl's death were laid out on both sides of the picture—and below, the caption that took Eddie's breath and didn't give it back for what seemed like a very long time. "The battered and sexually abused body of Angela Simm, aged eight, was found yesterday in a wooded area at the eastern edge of St. George's Island, not far from the zoo."

Still Eddie stayed and read. There were clippings spanning several months and they told the whole story. The murder had taken place in 1959, almost forty-five years earlier, and it had been savage. The killer had lured the girl away from a playground at the zoo not long before dark. No one knew at first what had happened to Angela Simm, just that she had disappeared. Hundreds of searchers combed the area, but the girl's body wasn't found for two days.

More than five hundred people attended the funeral, most of whom never knew Angela Simm. The killer remained at large for several months. He was eventually caught, but not before he had killed another girl, this one in Saskatchewan. The news of his capture was cause to interrupt a baseball game at Calgary's old Buffalo Stadium on a Sunday afternoon. The public-address announcer broke the news to the crowd and the game was held up for almost ten minutes as people stood and applauded. The murderer had quickly been found guilty and sentenced to life. He died of undetermined causes after only three years in prison.

It was all there. The reporters had obviously worked hard on the story and they left little untold. The Simm family had lived in Bridgeland for a dozen years. Eddie noted the address and calculated that it couldn't have been more than a few blocks from where Jack Simm lived now. Mr. Simm had been a salesman; he and his wife had four children—two sons and two daughters. Angela was the second youngest.

There was another photograph, also from a newspaper, that forced Eddie to look at it again and again. And each time he looked, Eddie felt his eyes fill with tears, even though it was the only picture Angela Simm was not in. It had been taken only days after Angela's body was found. It looked as if the photographer had asked the family to pose in the living room of their home. And on the far right, trying to smile as he must have thought you were supposed to when you were having your picture taken for the newspaper, was Angela Simm's older brother—twelve-year-old Jack.

Ten

Eddie lost track of how long he walked. He made his way slowly and aimlessly through the neighbourhood. A couple of times he realized he was making a second or even third trip up the same street. He had intended to check out the infill on his way back to the zoo—the one he planned to break into later—but after his visit to Jack Simm's house, he didn't feel like doing much of anything.

He did eat the banana, mostly because he was starving, but he didn't enjoy it. He wished now he hadn't taken it. Somehow, taking something even as insignificant as one lousy banana from Jack Simm seemed as wrong as anything Eddie had ever done in his life.

He finally decided not to go straight back to the zoo. He wanted to do some thinking and he wanted to do it somewhere other than where he had spent almost all of his time since he'd run away. He remembered that there was a little strip mall not far away. He'd walk there and rip off something to eat, or pay for it if he had to. But he wanted something good. Not good like in *good for you*, just good. Ice cream, maybe. Yeah, maybe a Fudgsicle. He'd loved those when he was a little kid and he couldn't remember the last time he'd had one.

He tried to think as he walked, but he wasn't sure what he wanted to think about. How could a person even begin to understand what Jack Simm must have felt when his sister was murdered? One of the newspaper clippings had said Jack was twelve at the time of the murder. Twelve years old. Eddie tried to remember back to when he was twelve. That was three years ago. Too long ago to remember a lot of it. Was he twelve when they did their first B and E? No, he was pretty sure he was thirteen. What was he like when he was twelve? He couldn't say for sure, but he thought he still believed that things were going to get better in his life. That all the bad stuff was just temporary. Oh, yeah, and he still thought he would play in the NHL.

He'd been wrong about both things. Life didn't get better, it got worse. And as for the NHL, he didn't even play hockey anymore. He'd quit the year after Steve moved in. It wasn't a whole lot of fun hearing your substitute old man yelling at you from the bleachers if you messed up on the ice.

Eddie wondered what Jack was like when *he* was twelve. Whatever kind of person he had been—whatever he thought about, whatever his dreams were—Eddie figured it all must have changed completely after what happened at the zoo. But he still didn't understand why Jack came to the zoo every day. What was that all about? Was it some kind of tribute to his little sister, some promise he'd made to himself not to forget her? Even if that was it—which would be weird enough after all these years—how did watching little kids at the playground fit in?

Ahead, the lights of the strip mall came into view. Eddie was glad. Thinking about all of this was giving him a headache. He decided to concentrate on how good the Fudgsicle would taste. But even that thought didn't cheer him. He knew he was down to less than two dollars, and, if he couldn't steal it, the Fudgsicle would take close to half of that.

As he crossed the parking lot to the gaudily lit convenience store, he caught a break. Not a big break, but they all counted. There was a quarter lying on the pavement. He scooped it up and dropped it into his pocket. Now even if the clerk was more alert than most, at least part of the Fudgsicle's cost was covered. Eddie shook his head. "This is nuts," he said out loud. "I'm getting excited about finding a lousy quarter, for God's sake." He looked around to see if anyone was close enough to hear him talking to himself. No one was and he opened the door and stepped into the store.

"Hey, how ya doin'?" a much-too-cheery clerk with acne and Lyle Lovett hair greeted him. The clerk didn't look much older than Eddie.

Eddie managed a weak smile. "Okay," he said.

Except for the clerk, Eddie was the only one in the store. He looked out into the parking lot. No one else on their way in, no one to distract the clerk. He wouldn't be able to rip off the ice cream. He went to the freezer and pulled a Fudgsicle from a cardboard box that had only three left. The Fudgsicle seemed smaller than Eddie remembered. He took it to the counter and paid without bothering to return the clerk's happy grin.

Eddie walked out into the parking lot and removed the wrapper. He stared at the frost-covered ice cream. He was sure now. There was a lot less to a Fudgsicle than there used to be. More cutbacks. He dropped the wrapper in a happy-face garbage can. After all the stuff he'd done, and all the trouble he'd been in, Eddie had never been able to shake the messages his grade-one and -two teachers had drilled into him about littering.

He ate slowly, wanting to make the moment last. It was a cool day so at least he didn't have to worry about the Fudgsicle melting. He started down the sidewalk of the strip mall and stopped in front of a used-furniture store with a television set playing in the front window. There was a speaker hooked up to the outside of the store, so Eddie decided to watch for a while. It had been a long time since he'd seen any TV.

It looked like the news was on. A female reporter was interviewing two guys. They both looked familiar to Eddie. They were talking about the economy. An election had been called—Eddie had seen that in a newspaper someone had left behind at the zoo—and these two men were candidates. The first guy's name came on the screen below his face. *The Honourable Arthur Hubley*. He was already in the government, a hotshot cabinet minister who was close to the premier. Eddie remembered that Hubley had been some kind of television evangelist before he got into politics. He appeared to be right at home looking into the camera.

"Bringing the deficit under control was God's will and the will of the electorate . . ." Hubley smoothed his tie as he talked. There were pictures of clouds and birds on the tie. "A few left-wing whiners have complained about what we've done, but we're not in government to serve whiners and special-interest groups. And here's something else you should know . . . for every complaint that comes in, my office receives at least three calls complimenting this government on its record of fiscal responsibility."

The reporter looked at the second man. "It's been said by some that business is the biggest benefactor of the government's current fiscal policy, and that those with average and low incomes have been made to suffer. As a candidate in the upcoming election, how would you answer a charge like that?"

The man changed positions a couple of times before speaking. "I am among those who have applauded the government for eliminating waste and holding the line on spending. Everybody, and I do mean everybody, should be willing to make some sacrifice so that this province and this country can get their financial houses in order." Below the man's face, his name appeared on the screen. *Wallace Pagler, Financial Consultant.*

Eddie almost dropped what was left of the Fudgsicle. Pagler! Sure. Eddie remembered him now. He'd seen him on TV before. This was Stink Pagler's old man. Eddie could see the resemblance. The features were similar and the meanness that showed in Stink's eyes was in his father's, too. Eddie had to admit that Stink's dad had it all over his kid in the dental department though.

Pagler looked a little uncomfortable as the reporter asked him to detail the financial sacrifices big business had made. She made the point that many corporations had downsized and maintained or increased their profits while eliminating the jobs of hundreds of employees and increasing the workloads of others.

Pagler looked into the camera and then just slightly away. "Business has had to do its part in fighting the deficit battle. We are fortunate to have a government that showed us the way and if I'm elected I will be proud to be a part of that continuing effort," he said.

Eddie pointed his Fudgsicle at the TV. "Mr. Pagler," he said aloud, "now I know why your kid is such an asshole."

It was getting late and Eddie thought he better start back to the zoo. On the way, he'd go by the infill. He couldn't put it off any longer.

He walked faster now. It helped him to stay warm as the evening air cooled with the setting of the sun on the western horizon. It was behind the skyscrapers of downtown Calgary now and Eddie cursed himself for not bringing his new ski jacket.

When he got to the street he slowed his pace. The house was the fourth one from the corner. The metallic-grey Jeep Cherokee was in the driveway. The living-room drapes were open and the light was on. Eddie allowed himself a little smile. It was like these people were inviting him to do their place. They were certainly being helpful. He could see the living room and a hallway he guessed led to the kitchen. No one was in the living room, although the television was on, and Eddie was able to take his time. The whole house had the look of money about it. That was good, very good. No point in going to the trouble of a break-in if there wasn't the promise of a reasonable reward for the effort.

As he walked slowly past the house, he looked back and saw a window, probably the kitchen. There was no corresponding window in the house next door, which made it a good candidate for his entrance. At the end of the block he turned and walked to the alley that ran behind the house. He didn't go far into the alley; that was too risky. He walked along just enough to see the back-yard and to make a mental inventory of what he saw.

No garage, a couple of small trees, a kids' swing set and a deck with a barbecue and a couple of lawn chairs. Nothing that would offer cover, which brought Eddie back to the conclusion that the side window was his best bet. He could be seen from the street, but only if someone going by actually turned and looked at that exact spot. And he wouldn't be there long. The kitchen window was off the ground a few feet, but here again the people living in the house were proving to be good hosts. A metal stepladder lay against the far end of the deck. It always surprised him how many people left ladders in plain sight. He'd learned early that this was one of the first things a B and E artist looked for.

There was just one more thing to check out and he wouldn't be able to do that tonight. The swing set meant little kids lived in the house. He'd have to make sure there wasn't a babysitter at the house during the day. Or a stay-at-home dad. Eddie had seen the woman leave for work in the Jeep, but that was later in the morning. He hadn't seen any signs of life around the place after she'd left, but he'd have to make sure. He didn't want to drop through that window only to find himself face to face with a terrified babysitter or a large husband with a crowbar.

He was finished. He hated the term "casing the joint"—it sounded too gangster movieish. He preferred the term "reconnaissance." Anyway, he was finished with the house . . . for now. He decided he would move on the place in three days. That would be Friday, which was good. Friday was his lucky day. He based that conclusion on more than just superstition. Not much bad stuff had happened to him on Fridays. He'd even kept a chart of when he got beat up by Steve and it happened less on Friday than on any other day of the week.

It had been a tough day and suddenly Eddie felt as tired as he had in a long time. He hadn't been able to get the pictures he'd seen in Jack Simm's bedroom out of his head.

As he retraced his steps back to the zoo—careful to keep his head down just in case the cops drove by—he thought. He thought about death. It seemed to Eddie that there had been an awful lot of death in his life so far. When he was in grade five, two of his school classmates died only a couple of months apart. One had some rare form of cancer. The other was killed in a car accident. The second kid's older sister and an aunt who was driving the car were killed, too. They were hit by a drunk driver who ran a stop sign. The newspaper said the guy was going over one hundred and twenty clicks on a residential street when he broadsided them. And while lots of kids had two sets of grandparents or at least one, Eddie didn't have any. They'd all died when Eddie was small. And now there was this thing with Jack Simm's little sister.

Sometimes it seemed to Eddie that death was all around him. Of course, the death Eddie thought about most often was his dad's. He thought about it again right then and he wished the same thing he did every time he remembered his dad's dying. Eddie wished that of all the people he knew who had died, he could have just one back. Even for a day.

Eleven

June 4, evening. I don't remember everything
about the day my dad was buried. And what I do
remember is stuff that isn't worth much, but
every time I think about that day it sort of
jumps out at me.

There was a fly. I couldn't see it at first,
but I could hear its buzz. It wasn't normal. It
was like the fly was stumbling along instead of
flying steady. Then I saw it. Up by the light. It
wasn't supposed to be there, not that day, not
just then.

"Too young to die." That was what everybody
said. They said it so many times I couldn't get
the words to stop buzzing around in my head.
Buzzing. The fly moved over to the window. I
was wishing that someone would open the window
and let it out. I kept watching the fly and
listening to its soft droning and its body hitting
up against the glass. I didn't hear much of what
Reverend Whitaker was saying. Except I heard
when he said my dad was too young to die.

I wished someone would let me out, too. I
hated the little room they put us in. And I hated
the curtain that was stretched across in front of
us. It was white and I could see through it, but

everything was fuzzy, so I couldn't make out the faces of the people who were there. About the only thing I could see clearly was the coffin.

I wasn't supposed to call it a coffin. Everybody else called it a casket. I guess that's supposed to be a nicer word or something. But at the time I didn't much care about the nicer words for everything about dying. I just wanted somebody to tell me how we were going to go camping without my dad to take us.

Coffin. Casket. Coffin. It didn't matter.

As I was sitting there, I had this sudden and really clear memory of my dad. Not of him exactly, but of something he used to say. I was afraid of the dark when I was little. Not just a little bit afraid, either. I was pretty much terrified. On those nights that I lay in my bed crying, my dad would come in and sit on my bed. He wouldn't say much. Most of the time he'd just sit with his hand on my shoulder and I'd feel better just having him there. But before he'd leave he'd always say, "I'm here, Eddie. Always and always." That was the part I liked, the "always and always" part. Hearing those words made me feel that no matter how scared or alone I was, my dad would be a part of me forever.

The fly was still after a while, not pestering the glass anymore to get out. I figured it must have given up.

The funeral was in Long Prairie, not far from the house where we used to live. I think my dad would have liked the idea of being buried there and not in the city. After he was buried, everybody went over to the Elks Hall for some lunch. People kept coming by where my mom and I were sitting to tell us how sorry they were and to give us hugs and pats. A couple of my aunts and some of our old neighbours had made sandwiches and little cakes and stuff. I asked Mom if I could go for a walk and she said I could. I went to the park.

The park was only two streets over and when I got there, the place was pretty well empty. In fact, the only person I saw was Mrs. Clara Campbell. She was sitting on the bench with the faded paint, right next to the tallest cottonwood tree in the whole park. I knew it had to be between three and four o'clock because Mrs. Clara Campbell always went to the park right at three o'clock and left exactly at four. Even though we'd been gone for two years, that part of life in Long Prairie hadn't changed. And she always sat on the bench with the faded paint right next to that big cottonwood. Everybody who had ever lived in the town knew about Mrs. Clara Campbell in the park.

Just like they knew Mary Jo Bender and Rory Wenzel met every night under the railroad bridge and did it on the grass next to the creek. And everybody knew that Gerald Coflin was the one who took Mr. Barnaby's Datsun and parked it on the front steps of the school for April Fool's. There's stuff you know when you live in a place.

Sometimes Mrs. Clara Campbell read while she was at the park. Sometimes she just sat and looked straight ahead. There were lots of things to see in the park, the kind of stuff you'd think an old lady like Mrs. Clara Campbell would have liked. There were squirrels, lots of them; there was the fountain with the boy and the trumpet that spouted water; and there were even some nice flowers here and there. But Mrs. Clara Campbell never looked at any of those things, at least not any of the times I'd seen her. She read or she looked straight ahead. And straight ahead from where Mrs. Clara Campbell sat on that bench, there wasn't anything at all to see.

I never heard her called anything but Mrs. Clara Campbell. I don't remember anybody ever saying Clara or even Mrs. Campbell. A lot of

times when us kids said it, we made it sound
funny with singsong voices or whiny voices or
some other voices that were meant to make fun
of her. But even when we were making fun, we
called her Mrs. Clara Campbell.

A couple of times we talked about going to the
park—the whole gang of us—at about a quarter to
three and staying there until after three o'clock.
We wanted to see what she'd do if her bench was
taken when she got there. Kids think about stuff
like that during summer holidays. We talked about it
a few times, but we never did it.

I don't know why I wanted to talk to her that
day. I'd never spoken to her before. Maybe I did
when I was a real little kid and my mom drove us
into town and took me for a walk in the park.
Little kids aren't shy about things like talking to
old ladies. Even ones that are kind of crazy.

Mrs. Clara Campbell was supposed to be
crazy. That's what people said. Mostly it was
other kids who said it, so I didn't totally believe
it. I learned pretty early on that you can't
believe a whole lot of what kids tell you. Or
adults either.

I did believe it a little bit though. Because Mrs.
Clara Campbell did some strange things. I don't
mean always sitting on the same bench and always

arriving at the park at the same time of day. She did some stranger things than that. Once, she spent Christmas morning hoeing in the garden. She had to sweep the snow off first so she could see the dirt. Then she stood there for most of the morning jabbing away at the frozen ground.

We heard about it from Joyce Tanner, who lived in the next house over. My dad said it was just because she was so lonely, being all by herself at Christmas. You couldn't necessarily believe what my dad said either, because he always made excuses for people. To me hoeing in the garden on December 25 is goofy behaviour.

And that wasn't all. Another time, she got on the phone and called every single person in the area to tell them she had just seen the first robin of the year. People who lived in the country had party lines back in those days and a lot of them were ready to hang her from that tall cottonwood in the park for tying up the phone for most of the day. She just started at A and kept calling until she got through to everybody in the phone book.

After a few hours of it, word had gotten around. Some of the people who hadn't been called yet left their phones off the hook to dodge the call. But when they hung up their phones before they went to bed, it wasn't fifteen minutes before Mrs. Clara Campbell had them on the other end of the line telling them about that bird. That happened when I was only two or something, but I remember people still talking about it when I was quite a bit older.

So she was crazy all right, at least some of the time. But I still wanted to talk to her. I just felt like it. Not because she was lonely. Who knows? Maybe she wasn't. I wanted to talk to Mrs. Clara Campbell for me, not for her.

"Mrs. Clara Campbell?" I spoke softly so I wouldn't scare her.

"I know you, Master Eddie Slater," she said, which I thought was kind of a strange way to start a conversation. And nobody had ever called me "Master" before.

"Yes, ma'am." I came around the bench and stood where she could see me if she turned her head a little ways to the left. She didn't though, just kept looking straight ahead like always. "I heard about your father." Her voice didn't sound like any of the ones we used when we were making fun of her.

"Yes, ma'am. The funeral was today."

"Yes."

She didn't say he was too young to die or he was a fine man or any of the other stuff people had been saying to my mom and me all day long. In fact, "yes" was the last thing Mrs. Clara Campbell ever said to me about my father dying.

It might sound strange, but she was pretty in a way, which you don't really expect in old people. She was quite small and thin, but her skin was mostly smooth and her eyes seemed clear and sharp—like she could see as good as anybody if her head hadn't been stuck in that one spot. She had on a light blue skirt and a little jacket thing that matched it. The skirt was fairly long. It almost made it to the ground.

I thought she must be kind of hot with that jacket on. I noticed that there was a little bit of moisture on her upper lip. That reminded me that I was kind of hot myself from having to wear a tie and have my shirt buttoned all the way to the top. I took off the tie and shoved it in my pocket.

One thing about Mrs. Clara Campbell not turning her head to look at you, it was kind of handy if you wanted to stare at her. That's what I was doing. Even with that drop of sweat on her lip, I still thought she looked very clean. From where I was standing, she smelled like flowers and apples. But maybe that was just the park.

I thought I should say something else and I wanted to talk to her some more, but I couldn't think of anything else to say. I guess I wasn't used to having conversations with people like Mrs. Clara Campbell.

I was starting to think about going somewhere else when I noticed her eyes flick a little in my direction. Not all the way so she was looking right at me, just a little closer to where I was standing. Then she said:

"He clasps the crag with crooked hands;
Close to the sun in lonely lands
Ringed with the azure world, he stands.

The wrinkled sea beneath him crawls;
He watches from his mountain walls,
And like a thunderbolt he falls."

Mrs. Clara Campbell's eyes flicked back to straight ahead when she finished.

"That's . . . a nice poem, Mrs. Clara Campbell, real nice. Did you write it?"

The funny thing was, I actually did think it was a nice poem. I didn't know exactly what it was about, but I liked it. And I liked that Mrs. Clara

Campbell just up and started reciting a poem the way she had. I remember thinking that was kind of special.

"No," she said, her eyes still not moving. "Tennyson."

"Oh, yeah," I said real fast, like I'd actually heard of the guy. It was a few years before we read any of Tennyson's poems in school. "Well, you sure said it nice."

And for the first time I saw Mrs. Clara Campbell smile. It wasn't a big smile, but it was enough to make me feel that maybe I'd said the right thing. I got to wondering if the books she always read when she came to the park were poetry books. I didn't know anybody who read poetry, not even my dad who had liked to read a lot.

That was the first time I had thought about my dad for a while. When I'd been talking to Mrs. Clara Campbell, I kind of forgot to think about him. I wasn't sure if that was a proper thing to do on the day he was being buried. I had plenty of time to wonder about it because Mrs. Clara Campbell didn't say anything more. Not for a long time.

I started to feel pretty stupid standing there right next to her, neither of us saying anything, but she didn't seem to mind. My legs began to hurt because I was keeping them real tense. I guess I was sort of nervous. I figured it was my turn to say something, but I wasn't sure how to talk to somebody who spoke in poems.

"I guess I should be going, Mrs.—"

"It's about an eagle." She said it so sudden, it made me jump. "Tennyson was writing about an eagle. Or had you figured that out?"

"Uh . . . no, ma'am. I mean, I wasn't exactly sure . . ."

"I hear you're something of a writer yourself, Master Slater."

"Well . . . uh . . . not really, no, I wouldn't say I was." I knew what she was talking about. I'd won an essay contest for the children and grandchildren of war veterans a couple of months before. I got fifty dollars for a prize and they put my picture in the Long Prairie paper—one of those former-resident-of-the-town-does-such-and-such stories. I guess that's how she knew. To tell the truth, I had spent a lot of time wishing I hadn't won that contest. When I got to school the day after my picture was in the paper, a lot of the kids were all over me about being a sissy writer. I wound up fighting a kid named Clark Morrison. He beat me up pretty good, but at least it got the rest of them off my back about that essay. I was hoping everybody had forgotten about it by now.

"Yes, I understand you're a very good writer, Master Slater, very good."

For the first time since I'd won the stupid contest I actually felt good about it. I mean, I was kind of excited when I first saw the words I'd written on the page of the veterans' magazine, but that wore off pretty quick once I got to school. In a way, I couldn't really blame the kids for saying all the stuff they'd said. It was just an essay. It wasn't like I'd scored the winning goal in a hockey game or something. I figured I wouldn't bother writing anymore.

Of course, my parents and my teacher were all excited about me winning, but you'd expect that. Mrs. Clara Campbell was the only person other than them who really seemed to think that being good at writing was okay.

"About your great-grandfather, I believe, is that correct?"

"Yes, ma'am. He was killed at a place called Vimy Ridge."

"Yes, I knew him." For a minute I thought she was going to turn her eyes my way again, but she didn't. "Well done, Master Slater, well done."

This time she didn't wait as long before she started talking again. "There were eagles here once." And just as easy as anything she tilted her head upward, as if to look at the place where they had been. I'd already decided there was something wrong with her neck, so I was a little surprised at how easy she moved it.

I looked up to where she was looking. "Oh," I said.

"Many years ago. Hundreds of them. Bald eagles. Goldens. They passed through here in the spring on their way to the summer nesting grounds in the North. I loved to watch them. They'd stop off here for a month or so in March and into April. That was before it got built up around here. They still come though, did you know that? They still come in the spring and they still stay for a month. But not here. South and west of here. They still come."

"That must be—"

"Have you ever seen an eagle?" Her head was still tilted up and she was squinting like the sun was hurting her eyes. It seemed pointless to me to stare off at where the eagles used to be but weren't anymore.

"No, ma'am. Except in pictures and on TV. Seen lots of hawks and some owls. Before we moved to the city. But no eagles. Not yet."

"No," she said.

I figured that was the end of our chat. I stood there a while longer in case she wanted to tell me anything else about eagles or recite another poem. But she didn't.

"Well, bye," I said. "It was nice talking to you." She brought her head back down then and I wasn't sure, but I thought she nodded just the littlest bit. I turned to leave.

I wasn't sure what I was going to report to the other kids about my conversation with Mrs. Clara Campbell. Some of the kids I had known when we lived in Long Prairie had come to the funeral and were probably still at the Elks Hall, loading up on the sandwiches and stuff.

I didn't know if I could tell them whether she was crazy or not. Talking about eagles and stuff that happened a long time ago didn't prove anything. That's what old people did. Of course, the way she talked about things was a little strange, what with the poems and not saying anything at all for a long time and never looking at you. But I still couldn't say for sure if Mrs. Clara Campbell was actually crazy. I decided it might be best not to say anything at all about talking to her. At least not right away.

I'd only gone a few steps when her voice stopped me. "Adventure," she said.

I stopped and looked back. She was turned completely around on that bench, staring right at me. Her eyes were narrow, like two small lights shining out of her face. Shining right at me.

"At the end of the summer, I am going to take part in an adventure," she told me. "I'm going to the northern tip of British Columbia to a place where eagles, hundreds of them, stay all year-round."

"That sounds really nice."

Then she said what I figured was the strangest part of our talk. "Have you ever had a real adventure in your whole life, Master Slater?"

I didn't get a chance to answer because Mrs. Clara Campbell got up from the bench and started off in the same direction she always went when she left the park. I looked at my watch. Four o'clock.

Mrs. Clara Campbell never got to that place to see the eagles. She died a few weeks before she was supposed to go. Mom told me that when people went into Mrs. Clara Campbell's house to take care of her stuff they found a copy of my essay taped onto her fridge door.

It still seems odd to me that the thing I remember most about the day of my dad's funeral was that time with Mrs. Clara Campbell. That and the fly.

Twelve

It would rain that day.

Eddie could feel it before he crawled out of the condo, even though he couldn't see the sky. It felt early, too, though he couldn't tell for sure. That was one more thing he'd forgotten when he took off . . . a watch. He hoped he could pick one up in the B and E; it would be nice to know the time without having to stare at strangers' arms or into office windows.

He didn't feel like going into one of the buildings to get warm so he walked instead. After a while he felt better, not chilled anymore. He sat down on one of the park benches and watched the traffic go by on the street that ran along the south border of the zoo.

He felt the presence of someone beside him before he heard or saw the person. Eddie turned his head slowly to the left. Jack Simm was no more than an arm's-length away. He was poking a stick at the ground and staring at Eddie. He didn't say a word.

"You ever just walk up to somebody *without* sneaking up on them?" Eddie let his voice show his displeasure at the intrusion.

"It's pretty hard to knock," Jack replied.

Eddie nodded but didn't say anything more. He wondered what had brought Jack to the zoo this early. Jack poked the ground a while longer then looked up. "If you're awake, let's go."

Eddie didn't move. "Where?"

"Let's go," Jack repeated. He dropped the stick on the ground and started walking. For the first time Eddie noticed that Jack had a bit of a limp. He guessed the old man might get stiff on cool, damp mornings like this one. Probably arthritis or one of those other things people Jack's age always seemed to talk about.

Jack didn't look back. It was like he knew that you'd do what he expected you to do without a lot of fuss. Eddie splashed some water from a drinking fountain onto his face and stood up. *All right*, he thought, *I'll play your little game just to see what this is all about.* Besides, there was always the chance that Jack would buy him breakfast. Which would be just fine.

But this didn't have anything to do with breakfast. Jack was walking fast, stiffness or not, and Eddie had to hurry to keep up. It was like when you were little and you had to sort of walk-trot to keep up with your mom when she took you shopping. Except this wasn't shopping and it wasn't his mom and Eddie was getting impatient. He stopped.

"This is as far as I go until I get some more information," he called ahead to Jack, who hadn't slowed down.

Jack stopped then and looked back. "It isn't far now," he said and began walking again.

That was a lie. They walked for a long time, long enough to end up in a part of the zoo Eddie had never seen before. In fact, he wasn't sure they were actually *in the zoo* anymore. Finally Jack stopped, allowing Eddie to catch up. As Eddie struggled to catch his breath, he noticed that Jack was breathing normally. The old guy might be a little stiff, but he was in damn good shape, Eddie decided.

A long minute passed before Jack pointed.

"What are we looking at?" Eddie asked. "All I see is freeway."

"The edge of the freeway—the edge nearest us—that clump of brush straight ahead. You see it?"

"Yeah."

"That's where they found my little sister. Right there . . ." He paused before adding, "You wanted to know about it. You might as well know all of it."

So that was it. Jack knew Eddie had been in his house. But how? Eddie decided not to ask. He also decided not to play dumb. They both knew. This wasn't the time for stupid denials.

"I'm sorry," Eddie said. "I wasn't trying to . . . invade your privacy or anything. I didn't know anything about you. And I wanted to. I mean, you have to admit it's pretty weird—this guy comes to the zoo every day for all these years and spends most of his time watching little kids at the playground. Hell, I didn't know what you were all about."

Jack leaned back, half sitting on a boulder. He looked at Eddie, then closed his eyes. "It was my fault," he said in a voice Eddie could barely hear over the freeway noise. "I was supposed to be watching her. But my friends and I were playing kick-the-can. When I went to find her she was gone . . . I was supposed to watch her and I didn't . . . and a sick son of a bitch came along and got her out here and . . . Those clippings didn't tell everything that guy did to my sister. You want to know that, too?"

"No . . . no, I don't."

"But I'll bet you want to know why. Why I sit there watching those kids every day, don't you? Maybe you think I'm just as weird as the guy that brought my little sister right over there and strangled her after he'd . . ."

Jack still hadn't opened his eyes and Eddie knew he was seeing it all over again, just the way it had been all those years before.

"Mom and Dad, they looked for her all that night and the next day. The police searched, the neighbours did, too. And lots of people we didn't even know. It took them two days to find her. My mom was never right after that. She died a few years later, mostly because she just didn't want to live. My dad tried, but he wasn't the same either. The rest of us kids, we got sent to B.C. to live with my aunt. That was better in a way. At least out there not many people knew us. When we still lived here, I bet somebody said something every day. 'Simm,' they'd say. 'I know that name. Are you related to that poor child?' Most of them knew before they asked, but they had to ask anyway."

Jack opened his eyes but didn't look at Eddie. Instead, he stared off at the place where Angela Simm had died all those years before. But Eddie wasn't sure that Jack was seeing the place just then. Or that he was seeing anything except maybe the pictures in his mind.

"I tried working at a couple of jobs out at the coast, but I could never stop thinking about it. There wasn't a single minute of the day that I didn't remember. But even so I started to think I was going to be okay. Then I got a job on the ferries going between Vancouver and Victoria. I liked the job. I liked the sea.

"One day a guy from Calgary got on the ferry. He knew me, at least he knew my family and he recognized me. We weren't five minutes away from the dock when he came up to me to tell me how sorry he was about what had happened. And that I shouldn't blame myself. His saying that made me realize that the whole damn world knew I was supposed to be looking after my sister that day.

"I knew I had to do something—I wasn't sure what, but something—or go crazy. There was a war on. Vietnam. I thought maybe going someplace far away and shooting people I didn't know anything about might somehow help . . ."

They were both quiet for a time. Traffic sounds surrounded them and a jet flew low overhead on its descent into the airport.

"Did it?"

Jack took a long time answering. It was if he'd forgotten Eddie was there.

"No," he said in the same low voice. "It didn't help. When I got back I mostly just wandered around. Did enough to eat every day and have a place to sleep. Not much more. Then one day it came to me. I knew exactly what I had to do. I had to come back here and sit by that playground and make sure nothing like what happened to my sister ever happened again. It isn't the same play-ground—they pulled that down a long time ago—but it's close to the one where . . ."

Jack closed his eyes again. Eddie looked to see if he was crying, but he wasn't. Maybe after a while you stopped crying—even after something as awful as what had happened to Jack. Eddie couldn't think of anything to say. He couldn't think of any words that could possibly make a difference or even make sense.

And he didn't understand, either. He didn't under-stand how a person's guilt could be so great that he would give up his own life to sit at that playground all those days, all those years. Surely no one could ever have blamed Jack for what happened? But maybe it didn't matter. Not if you blamed yourself.

Jack stood up and began walking back the way they had come. Eddie figured Jack wouldn't want him along, so he stayed where he was, looking at the ground. He was afraid to look up in case his eyes strayed back to that place by the freeway.

Jack stopped and turned back. "Don't ever break into my house again," he said, his voice only slightly louder than it had been. "You want to know something, you ask." He turned and Eddie watched him disappear around a bend and behind some trees.

Thirteen

The B and E was easy, almost as easy as getting into Jack's place. The ladder was still leaning against the deck, and the window had been no problem. But Eddie didn't like being there. In fact, halfway through, he wished he was somewhere else, doing something else. It was the first time since he'd started stealing that he'd felt that way.

He kept telling himself that without this stuff, he'd eventually starve. He'd waited until he was down to $1.11, so this wasn't an exaggeration. He'd had to do something, but he was hating every minute of it. For one thing these people seemed really happy. There were pictures all over the walls of them doing things together. In every one, they were smiling—real smiles, the kind Eddie remembered from when he was little and his dad was still alive.

Eddie recognized the woman and the little girl. He'd seen the woman twice before—the first time he'd checked the place out and again this morning as he'd watched the house from well down the street. The woman and the little girl had driven off in the Jeep Cherokee. A few minutes later, a man rode away from the house on a bicycle, brief-case in hand. *Health type*, Eddie smiled to himself, *granola and sunscreen*. Eddie couldn't tell for sure if the man on the bike was the one in the pictures—his face had been hidden by his helmet as he rode away—but Eddie was willing to bet the whole $1.11 that it was. This didn't look like a family that had a stepfather on the scene. No Steve here. Eddie forced himself to turn away from the pictures.

He decided to check out the master bedroom first. Experience told him that was where the best stuff would be—stuff he could carry and stuff that would have some value on the street. The three guiding words to a B and E artist were "cash," "jewelry" and "electronics." All three were easy to handle, were easy to dispose of and usually had some value.

Eddie's decision was a good one. Almost the first thing he spotted was a man's wristwatch, an expensive one. He checked it for engraving. You might get a decent dollar for something with initials, but not nearly as much as if the item was clean. This watch had no engraving. Eddie stuffed it in his pocket (he'd remembered to wear clothes with lots of pockets).

A few more pieces of jewellery followed, then a curling iron, a clock radio small enough to fit inside his biggest pocket, a handful of CDs, a cell phone (a nice dollar there), another watch—this one with a cheap plastic strap, he'd keep it for himself—an electric razor, a few coins (a couple of bucks at the most) and a paperback book. It was a mystery by someone named Tony Hillerman. Bonus. The book was also for himself. He was getting a little light on reading material.

He left the bedroom and checked out the kitchen. He designated one pocket of his pants for food. He stuffed part of a loaf of bread, a bran muffin, two butter tarts and a coil of sausage in the pocket, then tied a six-pack of orange juice cartons to his belt. It was as he turned away from the fridge that Eddie got lucky. An envelope lay on the kitchen table, an envelope addressed to the gas company. It was worth a quick peek.

Bingo! Clipped to the bill inside the envelope were four twenty-dollar bills. Someone had probably intended to take the bill and pay it today but had forgotten it on the counter. Eddie laid a loud kiss on the money as he detached it from the bill. He bent down and loosened his running shoe. The money went in there, under his foot. Even if he was chased and had to ditch the rest of the stuff, he'd still have the money. He looked at the gas company statement. The name was Pargetter . . . Mr. and Mrs. Neil Pargetter. That's who lived here. He couldn't decide if it was better to know the name of the people you were ripping off or not.

Eddie took a green garbage bag out of one pocket and looked around. Small appliances were good. They were easy to carry and easy to fence. He started with a coffee maker and followed it with a toaster, an electric frying pan and an electric teakettle. He debated taking a set of ceramic mugs that sat on the kitchen counter. Finally he wrapped them in a towel and carefully lowered them into the bag. He allowed himself a little smile. He'd get money for the mugs *and* he could use the towel himself.

He hefted the garbage bag up and down, testing it for weight and to see that it wouldn't break before he got back to the zoo. It could take a few more items—if they were small. He set a Brita water filter into the bag and added an electric knife. That would do for the kitchen.

He was getting antsy to be out of there. It wasn't much of a haul, he realized, but it would keep him going for a while. And besides, he wasn't having any fun. *A couple more good pieces and I'm out of here*, he told himself. He wondered where these people kept their camera. Cameras generally brought decent coin and a family like this was likely to have a pretty good one. Maybe digital.

He glanced in the living room but decided to give it a miss. It was unlikely there would be anything portable enough for someone on foot to handle. Besides, the living-room window faced the street and the drapes were open. No sense taking unnecessary chances.

There were two more rooms, one was the little girl's bedroom, that was obvious, and the other was some kind of office. He was careful not to even step into the little girl's room. He figured she'd be scared enough just knowing that someone had been in their house; he didn't want to make it worse for her. He tried to laugh at himself for feeling that way. "You're getting soft in your old age," he told himself, but the laugh was forced.

As he was turning away from the bedroom, he spotted a Walkman on the girl's dresser. He stood looking at it for a long time. It would be so great to have a little music, especially at night in the condo. He was at the dresser in three strides. He tucked the Walkman carefully in the bag and left the bedroom without looking back.

He stepped into the office—desk, computer, printer, fax machine, some other stuff that Eddie didn't recognize (and was too big to carry), some bookshelves filled with books Eddie had no desire to read and . . . a camera. It was a beauty, a Canon with some kind of fancy-looking lens attached and another one lying beside it. Not digital but decent. Better than decent . . . perfect.

He picked it up and gave it a quick look. There was a partially used film in it. He studied the camera for a minute, then rolled the rest of the film through. He popped it out and left it lying where the camera had been. He hoped the people would appreciate the gesture. Better to have a few wasted pictures than no film and maybe some treasured photograph gone forever.

"Damn, I'm a nice guy," Eddie told himself as he lowered the camera and the extra lens into the garbage bag.

It was time to go. He decided to go out the back door. There was more chance of being seen, but the chances of getting away were a whole lot better than if somebody spotted you with your ass halfway down a ladder eight feet off the ground. He stopped at the doorway of the little girl's bedroom once more and looked, carefully averting his eyes from the dresser top with its telltale space where the Walkman had been.

As Eddie looked at the posters on her wall—she was obviously into rock stars and Disney movies—he thought back to the time when he was her age . . . and safe . . . and happy.

"Hang on to it, kid," he said out loud. "Hang on to it every day, and hope nobody takes it away from you."

Eddie turned away from the girl's bedroom. His heart stopped.

Later, he couldn't say exactly how long it had stopped for, but he was absolutely certain that at that moment, his heart stopped beating. And he yelled. Or maybe "yelped" was more accurate. Standing between Eddie and the back door—a door that now stood half-open—was a person.

He was a small person, but for at least a three count he was the scariest human being Eddie had ever laid eyes on—right up there with Stink Pagler or Ratsy. It was a few seconds before Eddie had recovered enough to properly assess his situation. The kid was maybe five years old, tops, maybe not even that. That was the good news. He wasn't likely to try to overpower Eddie. The bad news was that the kid was there at all. If he started yelling, he'd bring people from all over the place. Except he didn't look as if he was getting ready to yell. Mostly, he looked curious.

"Whooee—" Eddie tried to grin at the kid "—scared me there! I didn't hear you come in."

The boy kept looking at Eddie but didn't say anything.

"You . . . you live around here, don't you?" Eddie didn't want it to sound like too much of a question. Better to let the kid think he was familiar with the neighbourhood, like he belonged here.

The boy still didn't speak or move. Just kept watching Eddie. Finally his eyes moved from Eddie's face down to the green garbage bag. Eddie thought fast. Unless this kid was either stupid or had never seen any television, he was going to figure out pretty quick that the total stranger about to slip out the back door with a garbage bag in his hand probably wasn't an invited guest. Eddie had to do something.

"You friends with the Pargetters?" he asked, hoping the kid actually knew these people's last name.

The boy nodded, still looking at the bag. Finally his eyes drifted back up to Eddie's face. "You doing something for Cory's birthday party?"

Eddie could have kissed him. "Uh . . . yeah . . . I brought some stuff to hide . . . it's sort of a surprise . . . and . . . Cory's mom and dad, they wanted me to take some stuff to them to get ready for the party—" he gestured at the bag "—their camera and stuff, you know?"

The boy smiled a conspiratorial smile and nodded. "Want me to help you?"

"Oh . . . uh . . . thanks, but I'm pretty well finished. I should get this stuff to Mr. Pargetter's office. Should be a neat party, eh?"

"I got her a Barney backpack. You wanna come to my house for a juice box?"

"Hey, thanks . . . uh . . . what's your name?"

"James."

"Well, thanks, James, but I better not. How'd you get in here, anyway? I . . . uh . . . thought I'd locked that door behind me."

"It *was* locked. I got my mom's key. Cory's mom left a key for my mom cuz there's some present gettin' delivered today. They didn't tell me what it was. Do you know?"

Eddie shook his head. "But I'll bet it's a really neat one. Uh . . . so does your mom know you're over here?"

It was James's turn to shake his head. He looked at the floor. "I snuck the key off the table. I wanted to see if the present was here."

"Yeah, well . . . uh . . . James, you shouldn't be sneaking into people's houses, you know." Eddie had trouble getting that out without laughing. A lot of trouble. "Tell you what though. Want to play a game of hide-and-go-seek?"

"Sure!" the boy's freckled face lit up. "Who gets to hide first?"

"You can," Eddie told him. "But it has to be somewhere in the house, that's the rule. Okay, go, I'll count to twenty."

143

Eddie pretended to cover his eyes and watched through his fingers as James disappeared into the living room.

Damn, Eddie thought. *I should have made another rule, no living room.* ". . . sixteen, seventeen, eighteen, nineteen, twenty." He finished the count and started toward the living room, his eyes on the front window. Nobody going by on the street. He'd have to hope no one in any of the houses across the street had chosen this moment to look out the window.

"Hmm, I wonder where he went," Eddie murmured as he spotted a running shoe sticking out from behind the chesterfield. He pretended to look behind the TV, under a coffee table and all around the piano, even lifting the seat of the piano bench and peering inside. "Nope, not in here. I wonder where James went."

Then, when a decent amount of time had gone by, he pretended to stumble across James's shoe and the rest of James quite by accident. The boy giggled as Eddie pulled him out from behind the couch and tickled his stomach.

"Okay, it's my turn now. Do you know how to count to twenty?" Eddie asked.

"Sure." James nodded confidently. "I can count up to fifty a hundred million thousand."

"Yeah, well, that's real good, but twenty is probably enough. You have to count real slow and no peeking, okay?"

James nodded. "One . . ."

"Not yet," Eddie told the boy. "First get down there where you were hiding before and cover your eyes. I'll hide somewhere in the house. Remember . . . count real slow."

James dutifully crouched down behind the couch. Eddie could hear the count as he silently stepped into the kitchen and toward the back door.

"One . . . two . . . free . . . four . . . five . . . sammin . . . ten . . . four . . . sammin . . ."

There was no telling how long James would count before he got bored. Eddie hoped the kid's mother wasn't standing in the next yard looking for him. But he had no choice. He had to go and he had to go now. He slipped through the back door and gently closed it behind him. A quick look around told him all was okay for the moment.

He stepped down the back steps and held his breath until he got to the garage. Between the garage and a couple of good-size trees in the backyard he was pretty well shielded from the houses on either side. Once he was in the alley behind the house he started moving faster.

He figured it wouldn't be long before James got frustrated at not being able to find him and went home to tell his mother about the big boy he'd seen in Cory's house. What would be really funny was if the kid's mother didn't believe him. Or maybe James wouldn't tell because he'd also have to say how he knew about the big boy.

It didn't matter, Eddie realized, especially with the ladder leaning up against the house. He'd have to keep moving. He cut through another yard, crossed a street and changed directions again. He had already decided to take the long way back to the zoo. He preferred to stay around buildings for as long as he could. It would have been easier if the General Hospital was still where it had been for so many years. The rubble pile and open space wouldn't offer much cover. Still, he didn't have much farther to go. He was minutes away from succeeding in his first solo B and E. He felt exhilarated and allowed himself a little laugh.

But his mind's eye kept seeing the little girl's room with its pictures of rock stars and Disney movies on the walls and Eddie stopped laughing. He picked up the pace, using a sort of jog-trot a lot of the time. He wasn't sure how long it would be before the robbery was reported or when the cops would respond to the call, but he wanted to be back at the zoo before it happened.

The worst part was the open space—probably the equivalent of several blocks—he would have to cross between the last buildings of Bridgeland and the shelter of the park area that bordered the zoo. He slowed down a little for that, even though he didn't want to. He figured that even in the middle of the day, a kid running and carrying a garbage bag could look a little suspicious.

He heaved the garbage bag up over his shoulder. Trying for casual.

He reached the zoo and didn't slow down until he was through the hole in the fence and inside. Here he felt safe, not just from the cops, but from the whole world. He'd made it, and that was cause for celebration. After counting his money one more time, he decided he could afford a pop. Even though he had the six juice boxes, he wanted a pop . . . bad. He was thirsty and his mouth was dry although he knew it wasn't from the heat. He'd been scared, or at least nervous. In fact, he'd been feeling that way since last night. It was the first night since Jack had directed him to the condo that he'd had trouble sleeping.

Tonight would be different, he told himself. Tonight he would sleep like a baby. First, he'd stash the stuff he'd stolen in the same place he kept his extra clothes. Then he'd get that pop and sit down and write for a while. He hadn't found a flashlight at the house—one of the things he'd wanted most—but he could use some of the money to buy one, along with enough batteries to read the Tony Hillerman book and a bunch more.

He thought again about James, counting and trying to find him. And he laughed. This time he laughed so hard that tears rolled down his cheeks and along the corners of his mouth. It had been a good day. Yeah, it had been a real good day.

Fourteen

June 11, 12:45 P.M. (according to my new watch!).
A while back I started to write about what it
was like going to court and eventually to jail.
But then I started thinking and talking about
Ratsy and I never did finish putting down all the
gory details about being locked up. It was two
years ago. And it wasn't fun.

Whenever I think about going to court, I
remember it in numbers. Courtroom Four; two
rows of benches that reminded me of church
pews; twelve people sitting on those benches,
mostly looking straight ahead or at a notebook
of some kind; five microphones scattered around
the room; three guys in suits, two expensive-
looking, the other one looking as if it came
from one of those Goodwill stores (the suits
were doing a lot of talking and some laughing
at the long desk in front of the pews); four
pictures on the walls, two of them were of the
Queen; one cop, a lady you didn't fool with;
one judge; and one accused—me.

The accused: that's what they call you in
Courtroom Four.

This was the third time I had been to court—they
call these visits "appearances"—since I'd been

caught that second time. The first two times I was in and out of there in such a hurry I didn't really have time to figure out what was going on. My lawyer, he never explained much, just told me that the court was waiting on some report from a social worker before sentencing me. We had already decided—actually, the lawyer had decided—that we would plead guilty. That's how he put it . . . "we" would plead guilty. I felt like asking him how long "we" would be in the CYOC. Actually, I agreed with him about how we should plead. It would have been pretty stupid to plead not guilty when the cops caught us half a block from the house with two backpacks full of stolen stuff. Besides, I figured being in the CYOC would definitely be an improvement over being at home with Steve.

The other thing I remember about going to court was how nobody really looked at me and a lot of the time they talked about me as if I wasn't there. Then, just when I started to think that I might as well be back in the waiting room with all the other accused, the judge turned and actually did look at me.

He was supposed to be a good guy. His name was Windsor. The other kids at the remand centre (that's where they keep you while the court stuff is going on) told me I'd be all right if I got Judge Windsor. Of course, his name didn't matter. I'd been told to call him Your Honour if I actually got to talk to him . . . which I didn't. What mattered was that the guy didn't hate kids—at least that's what they told me. They said, "Get Judge Windsor, he's all right." Like I had any say in who would be sitting at the front of that courtroom.

Judge Windsor looked at me over the top of those half glasses some people wear. He didn't say anything right away, just looked. Like he was trying to figure out if he should talk tough or try the nice-guy approach. He didn't do either. He said he'd really like it if we didn't have to meet up this way anymore and he kind of smiled. I couldn't help liking the guy, even though he looked as if he could be tough enough if you made him mad.

Looking back on it, I think it must be a tough job being one of those judges. I mean, how is he supposed to know if I'm just a punk wanting to rip off a few people and piss off Steve, or if I'm somebody really scary like Ratsy or Stink Pagler. I guess that's what the report from the social worker was all about. Anyway, I got three months in the CYOC. That doesn't sound like much, but after you're in there a week, three months starts to feel like a couple of lifetimes.

At the CYOC I wasn't called "the accused" anymore. Now I was one of the "inmates." Personally, I'm not too crazy about either one of those names. Another thing I wasn't crazy about is that you couldn't keep any personal items with you. No wallet, no money, not even your own comb. They take those away the day you arrive. That first day isn't a lot of laughs, especially if you're a person who's used to privacy. They start you off with a strip, shower and cavity search. I didn't even know what a cavity search was. Now that I know, I'd like to go through the rest of my life without another one.

One of the first things I noticed about the place was the smell. It's pretty hard to miss. There are windows, but they don't open, so the whole place smells like a urinal most of the time.

There are seven units in the Centre and all of them are named after mountains around Banff. Like calling something Rundle or Assiniboine is going to make you feel like you're camping in the Rockies. I was in Yamnuska. That bugged me because I remembered going camping with my mom and dad at a campground right near Mount Yamnuska. Trust me, the unit wasn't quite like the real thing. My cell had two beds in it. There were no curtains, no wallpaper and no doors on the closets. There sure as hell weren't any movie-star posters on the wall either.

Sixteen rooms—eight on a top level and eight on a lower level—formed two circles around what's called "the pot." That's the control desk where a CYOC staff member (they don't like to be called guards) sits and watches the inmates on TV monitors. They can listen in to conversations, too. Actually, they aren't guards, but they are in constant radio and visual contact with security.

Some of the staff were pretty nice, but you got the feeling they didn't trust you at all. I guess I can't blame them. They'd probably been burned a few times. Some of the kids in that place tried to beat the system every way they could. I probably wouldn't have trusted us either.

Like I said, privacy isn't one of the CYOC's big selling features. That goes for the bathrooms, too. There's one for each level, and showering, bathing and taking a leak are public events. Phone calls are monitored, and if you get any mail—I didn't—they open it for you.

There's a solitary room if you get too far out of line. It's six feet by six feet with

concrete walls and a mat on a concrete floor. I
managed to stay out of that place. The TV
room, if you ask me, wasn't a whole lot better.
There was one black-and-white, twelve-inch
TV—I bet the only ones they still make are for
young offenders centres, and guys like Jack
Simm. The TV at the CYOC gets turned on only
at certain times of the day and there's no VCR.
One thing you do not want to do is get into an
argument about what show to watch. As soon as
that happens, the TV goes off and the arguers
are locked up in their rooms.

We did all our own laundry and all the cooking
and cleanup. That included cleaning toilets, not
one of my favourite jobs. There were other
chores, too. The better you got along with the
staff and the other inmates, the better chores
you got. I always got level-three and -four
chores (those are the good ones) because I
figured out right off that getting along with
everybody kept your hands out of the toilet
bowls and urinals.

I hated mornings there. First thing when
we woke up, we were sent in for showers then
breakfast. There was no such thing as taking a
nice long shower. We got out of our rooms
eight at a time and had to be showered, finished

breakfast and done brushing our teeth by 8:30 a.m. It was hard to make a fashion statement in there since all of us wore the same thing—navy blue sweatsuits and these stupid brown plastic sandals that made walking difficult and running just about impossible.

At 8:45 we started school, and that was different, too. In my high school there were some total jerks in just about every class. I never figured out how they got away with the stuff they did. In one class a kid called the math teacher an asshole. For that he got a three-day in-school suspension. We all laughed about that.

School at the CYOC wasn't like that at all. We sat down, we shut up and we worked. Any kid that tried to do the high-school routine with these teachers wound up locked in his room. And if that didn't work, it was isolation time. Even guys like Ratsy didn't screw around much in CYOC classes.

After school we did our chores and then we had some free time. There were a couple of pool tables, a Foosball table, a library, a computer lab, a woodworking shop, a home ec lab and a gymnasium. I hated going to the gym. There were always a couple of guys who got pretty rough in the basketball games. There's always at least one person who thinks every game is game seven of the NBA final. Can you say Stink Pagler?

Actually, the time Stink Pagler went wacko on me in the basketball game was about the only time anybody tried to get rough with me . . . in the gym or anywhere else. That's because everybody figured out I was friends with Ratsy, and once they figured that out, I didn't have much to worry about. I never saw Ratsy lay a hand on anybody. I guess he didn't have to. The whole time I was there, no one ever tried to find out how tough he really was.

If the weather was decent we went outside. I didn't like that much either, mostly because there was a fence around the yard with barbed wire running along the top. It looked like one of those prisons you see in movies. There's nothing like barbed wire to remind you where you are.

But the worst was at night. That's when you got locked in your room. Every time I heard that door lock I had this urge to run at it as hard as I could and try to break out. Of course, I wasn't stupid enough to actually do it, but God how I hated having that door locked with me inside.

My roommate (cellmate) was a kid named Jackie. He was in there for starting fires. He'd started a few pretty impressive ones. Nights were real tough on him. He told me he'd been sexually abused, like about half the kids in that place if the stuff you heard was true. I'm thinking it was. At night, Jackie would sometimes cry for a long time.

He wasn't very big—even smaller than me—and I think for the first month or so Jackie thought I was going to try something with him. Once he figured out that I wasn't interested in getting his pants off, he told me about the abuse. He didn't give any details and I didn't ask. I figured it was probably pretty hard for him to say even that much.

You want to know something weird? The closer I came to getting out, the more I started to like the place. Well, maybe not "like" exactly, but not hating it as much either. Of course, that was mostly because I knew how bad it was going to be when I got home. Actually, quite a few of the kids in there reoffend (that's the courtroom word for committing another crime) as soon as they get out, because for them home is a worse place to be.

For a while after I got out I figured there were only two choices—living at home with Mom and Conan the Barbarian, or breaking the law

until I got caught and sent back. Since I've
been at the zoo, it seems like there might be
another choice. Maybe without all that
excitement I talked about before—the big rush
when you do something illegal. I guess I
wouldn't hate it if my life didn't have that
anymore. I'm just not sure how I'm going to get
there. I still need money and I still need to eat.

But one thing being free and living at the zoo
has taught me: I don't want to go home and I
don't want to go back to the CYOC. Both of
those places are prisons, and prisons aren't fun.

Fifteen

Something was different. Eddie felt it even before he opened his eyes. Something was very different. Something was *wrong*.

One of the few disadvantages of the condo was that the tight quarters made getting dressed inside a challenge. And getting dressed quickly was pretty much out of the question. Even though Eddie wore a T-shirt and socks to bed, there was still the job of getting into his pants. A real shirt could wait until he was outside, but Eddie preferred to hit the open air with his pants on.

Most mornings this was no big deal—he had all the time in the world to snake his way into his pants. But today was different. Today he wanted to hurry. *What the hell was it?*

He didn't think he was imagining it. No, there was something about this morning that was different from all the others. Finally he was into his pants and ready to move outside. That's when he realized what was wrong. It was the ducks. They weren't making their usual little duck noises. And *his* duck—the one that was always looking at him when he woke up—she wasn't there.

The cops? That seemed impossible. He was sure he hadn't been followed. Had they been tipped off? And if so, by whom? Jack Simm? Eddie doubted that. Zoo security? Maybe they'd spotted him, or maybe Jack had told them about him. Eddie ruled out that last possibility. Jack wouldn't turn him in even if he was pissed off. That wasn't the way Jack Simm would handle things.

Eddie tried to look out. Another of the condo's disadvantages quickly became evident. Except for a very narrow strip above the opening that he used to get in and out of the place, visibility was pretty well nil. The only way he was going to find out what was going on outside was to go out there. He pulled the Swiss Army knife out of the ground and started out.

He hurried. Once out, he looked quickly at the pond. The ducks were out of the water, most on the far bank, not looking all that stressed and yet obviously not wanting to be any closer. Eddie looked right, then left. No one.

"Did I mention they let me in for free?" the voice came from behind him.

Eddie looked behind him. "This isn't Vietnam. You don't always have to sneak up on people."

Jack Simm smiled. "When I was a kid we all got in for nothing. That's why we came here to play. We had the world's greatest playground a ten-minute bike ride from home and it was free."

"What's the matter with you, man?" Eddie interrupted, staring hard at Jack's face. "You come up behind people like that, you gotta be nuts—"

"There was a lot more green space then. And a hell of a big playground. We loved it. That's where—" He stopped for a minute and looked away. "Now they have buildings representing every part of the world and just about every kind of animal. I guess that's the way it's supposed to be in a zoo, but I liked it better when there was lots of open space. People would come and just walk and lie on blankets and have picnics. You didn't have to look at animals the whole time. It was nice."

Eddie started to wonder if Jack had lost it. The man was having a conversation with himself! Eddie wasn't sure what he was supposed to say, or if he was supposed to say anything at all.

Jack looked at him. "It was you who broke into that house, wasn't it?"

Eddie started to pull on his shirt. "What?"

"The Pargetters. I've met them a couple of times around the neighbourhood. I heard some people talking about it last night in the grocery store. They said somebody broke in and stole a bunch of stuff. I figure it was you."

"Look, first you come sneaking around here, and the next thing, you're accusing me of stuff. I don't know what—"

"I brought you a coffee." Jack pulled a cup from the paper bag he was holding. He held it out to Eddie, then took another cup out of the bag for himself.

Eddie took the coffee. Jack had fixed it the way he liked it. It wasn't hot anymore, but it wasn't cold either and it was nice to have coffee first thing in the morning. Eddie could feel Jack watching him.

"You do drugs, kid?"

Eddie was surprised at the question. It had come with no warning, like a lot of things Jack Simm said. The man wasn't one to ease into a conversation, there was no doubt about that.

"No." Eddie took a sip of the coffee. It wasn't a total lie. He'd only smoked up a few times at parties and he sure didn't have extra money to buy anything right now. Actually, he'd been so busy just trying to survive that he hadn't given any thought at all to drugs. There were times he wouldn't have minded having a pack of cigarettes, but now that he had some money he could take care of that.

"There's no sense you and me BSing each other." Jack was stirring his coffee with a pen. "You get as old as I am, you figure out that BS is just about the biggest problem there is in this world. I'm just hoping you didn't steal that stuff so you could buy drugs."

"You seem to have a lot of things figured out." Eddie looked at Jack over the rim of his coffee cup.

"That's the second time you said that." Jack shook his head slowly. "I don't. But I'll tell you what I *do* know, kid."

"Yeah, that's just what I need—parental advice."

"Nothing parental about what I'm telling you. And that is that you're going to have a pretty crappy life if you keep going like you are."

Eddie looked away. He didn't feel like a lecture. Especially from someone who hung out at the zoo every day because he couldn't get his own life together.

"Right now, the people who run the world don't like to deal with people with problems," Jack said slowly. "They don't like it that there are poor people and sick people and old people. What they like is having a system where things go real nice for the people with money . . . so those folks can keep making more money without a bunch of hassle. And somebody like you—you're a hassle. Now, those same people—the ones that are running everything—they don't give two damns about how tough your life has been. Lots of people have tough lives . . . and they don't all end up being screw-ups. You better get your head around that little news flash real soon."

Jack sipped his coffee. Eddie noticed that the pen was still sticking out of the cup. He hated to admit it, but he found himself listening to what Jack was saying. He thought back to the television interview he'd seen with Stink Pagler's old man. Eddie figured Pagler and the other government guy fit in pretty well with Jack's theory. Even so, he hoped the speech wouldn't go on much longer. He wanted to enjoy his coffee without being called a screw-up by the most screwed-up person he'd ever met.

"I'm not planning to buy any drugs."

"Well, that's good." Jack nodded. "Doesn't matter much though. Do you know there are places in the world where they cut off your hands for stealing a loaf of bread to feed your family? We don't do that, so I guess that makes us civilized. But we think the same way about one thing.

Stealing is stealing, doesn't matter what your reason is. It's all about that system. The system is everything. And you're a drain on the system, same as that sick person or that old person. So something has to be done about you and all the other drains. And the easiest—and cheapest—thing to do is to concentrate on catching pups like you and kicking your butts around the block a few times."

"Who says I'm going to get caught?"

Jack took the pen out of his cup and threw the rest of the coffee away. He put the cup back in the paper bag. "I thought I was talking to somebody with a little intelligence. You saying something like that tells me I was wrong."

"Yeah, well, if all that stuff you said was right, then what's wrong with taking a few things back from the people with all the money?"

Jack shook his head. "First of all, the Pargetters aren't the people I'm talking about. They're just a young family busting their backsides to make an okay living. They're not the problem and they're not the ones the government is falling all over itself to look after. But even if they were, stealing their stuff just makes you as bad as the worst of them."

"Well, I'm not giving any of the stuff back, if that's what you came here for."

Jack stood up. "That's not what I came for." Jack stepped across the stream and over the wire fence on the other side. It was hard for him to lift his leg up that high and it took him a while to get solidly on the other side. He looked back at Eddie. "I like you, kid. I don't know why, but I do. And I don't want to read about you in the newspaper."

Eddie watched as Jack walked off in the direction of Dinny. The old man passed under the belly of the huge dinosaur and disappeared from view.

"Thanks a lot," Eddie said out loud, though he knew Jack was out of earshot. The old man had ruined his morning. Eddie didn't feel like thinking about all the stuff Jack had said. Not right now. Maybe not ever. "Nobody's out there worrying about me." He sent the words in the direction Jack had gone. "I'm the only one who's taking care of me. And that's just what I plan to keep on doing . . . old man." He said the last two words slowly and bitterly as he drained the last of the coffee. It was cold now and Eddie didn't like the taste it left in his mouth.

Sixteen

Jeremiah. Eddie couldn't remember the last name. He wasn't sure he'd ever heard it. But Jeremiah was the first name, he remembered that much.

Jeremiah was a fence. Eddie'd met him once before when he and two friends unloaded some stuff they'd stolen out of a parked car. The car had been in a mall parking lot and they'd broken into it in broad daylight. That particular job had scared the crap out of him and he didn't go along when the same two friends suggested that they try the same thing at a different mall a few weeks later. Saturday afternoon. Eddie heard later they had broken into a BMW. They'd been caught before they even got the radar detector unhooked. That got both of them a stay in the CYOC.

But right after that first car break-in, the three of them had headed over to Inglewood to move the stolen stuff. One of the guys, Terry Graydon, had dealt with Jeremiah before and knew where to find him. Terry said to let him do the talking. You had to say exactly the right thing—sort of like code.

To Eddie, the episode was like something out of a really dumb spy movie. They had gone to a new-and-used store on Ninth Avenue. It was one of the only crappy places left in that part of town. Inglewood was an old neighbourhood that had been rediscovered by the yuppies and was now dotted with trendy restaurants, coffee places and antiques stores.

Eastside New and Used wasn't in any of those categories. The place was filled with junk—to Eddie most of it seemed unusable. They had gone inside and Terry asked the guy behind the counter—you couldn't really call him a clerk—if he had any Fender guitars. The guy was about the greasiest person Eddie had ever seen. Not somebody you'd want to meet in a dark alley, or even a well-lit one.

The greasy guy looked at each of them in turn. "Acoustic or electric?" he asked. Terry said, "I want a red one." The sales guy wandered off, undoubtedly to a phone somewhere in the back, and after about ten minutes or so, Jeremiah showed up. As they were going through the little guitar charade, Eddie had almost burst out laughing. But he managed to hold it in. None of them knew another fence and they weren't sure how to find one.

Jeremiah was another story—a cross between a really old hippie and an undertaker from a western movie. He was tall, with a long beard that looked like something might have nested in it once. He was dressed in black: black jeans, a black Harley-Davidson T-shirt and black cowboy boots, the old kind with the really pointed toes.

They had gone in the back and done their dealing with Jeremiah. It was like a scene from the black-and-white version of *A Christmas Carol*, the one where the people who have stripped Ebenezer Scrooge's room of all his stuff are selling it to a crooked used-goods dealer. Eddie had been glad when they were out of the dumpy old store and a long way from Jeremiah. They hadn't gotten a lot of money for the stuff they'd stolen, and they'd blown all of it in a couple of days.

Now, Eddie wasn't all that excited about having to deal with Jeremiah again, especially by himself. But the only other way to get rid of the Pargetters' stuff was to hang out at some of the rougher bars and ask around until you found someone interested in taking something off your hands. That took too long and it was a little too dangerous. That made Jeremiah the only option.

Eddie decided to get it done right away. Jack Simm's morning chat had thrown him off a little and he just wanted the whole thing over as fast as possible.

He packed up what he'd stolen and headed for Inglewood, which lay in the opposite direction from Bridgeland. Eddie left the zoo through the main south entrance, quickly crossed a bridge and turned east so that he would be in a residential area for most of the walk to Eastside New and Used.

He hesitated for a few minutes outside the store, but when a police cruiser went by, Eddie hurried inside. The greasy guy had been replaced by a smaller, older guy who was almost as greasy. And even meaner-looking. This new element made Eddie uneasy. What if the guy was an undercover cop? He ruled out the idea right away. Not even the cops could have somebody like this on the payroll.

Eddie was still trying to decide whether to stay or go, when the guy spoke to him. "What do you need today?" The man sounded like he looked.

"Uh . . . I'm looking . . . uh . . . you got any Fender guitars?"

The guy grinned in a way that didn't make Eddie feel any better about being in the place. "Wanna coffee, friend?"

That wasn't the right answer. Had Jeremiah moved on? Was he hanging out somewhere else now? Hell, maybe he was in jail. Maybe this creep *was* undercover after all. Or an informer.

"No, thanks." Eddie shook his head. "Just wondering about Fender guitars."

"That so? My name's Jules." The man stuck out his hand. It was as dirty as the place.

Eddie didn't feel like shaking hands, but he couldn't turn and run for it either. He needed to move the Pargetters' stuff. He shook hands, and immediately thought about soap and water. Now Jules was standing closer than Eddie liked. Eddie took a step back.

"So . . . you interested in electric or acoustic?"

Okay. They were on the right track. But Eddie still had a feeling that this guy was playing some kind of game. "I'd like a red one," he said in a small voice.

"Good choice, friend. Real good choice. Your name wouldn't be Eddie, would it?"

"Uh . . . what . . . uh . . . no, you must be thinking of somebody else."

"Sure. I guess you just look like this guy named Eddie." Jules grinned again. "Well, here's the deal, friend. Turns out you came on a bad day. Jeremiah, he's . . . out of town just now. However, there's also good news, which is that you can deal with me. I'd be happy to help you out. I'll just put the 'Gone for Coffee' sign out and lock the door. Then we'll head into the backroom and conduct us a little business."

Eddie wasn't sure at all about going into the backroom with this creep. But Jules had already gone to the front of the store to lock the door. Eddie looked around. Behind him on a table was some camping gear, including a small hatchet for chopping firewood. Eddie unzipped his jacket, stuffed the handle of the hatchet down the front of his jeans so that the blade was just sticking out and zipped the jacket back up.

Jules returned from the front of the store. "Follow me. Right this way into my parlour, said the spider to the fly." Jules grinned again. "Just an expression, you understand."

When they were in the backroom, Jules set two wooden chairs across from each other and sat on the dirtiest one. He pointed at the other. "Go ahead, Eddie, have a seat. Let me see what you got."

Eddie didn't sit. He set the garbage bag on the chair and opened it up. Then he stepped back. "Help yourself."

As Jules rummaged through the bag and pulled things from it, Eddie looked around. The room was disgusting. It was the dirtiest place he had ever been in. Behind Jules was a dining-room table laid over on its side. It looked as if someone had been repairing or maybe refinishing it. Judging from the amount of dust on the table, Eddie guessed the work had taken place at least ten years before.

The rest of the room looked like one of those appliance stores that were always called Crazy Frank's or Crazy Bob's. There were hundreds of televisions, stereos, car radios and computers. But there was one thing that didn't fit. Near the back of the room was a car. Eddie couldn't tell what kind of car it was, thanks to the fact that it was almost buried in television sets. He also couldn't figure out how the car had gotten inside the building. There were no big doors anywhere that he could see.

Jules kept up a constant stream of muttering as he examined each article he took from the garbage bag. Eddie couldn't make out what the man was saying, and he wasn't about to get close enough to find out.

After a while, Jules looked up. "I'm figurin' you got maybe fifty bucks here."

"Get real, the camera's worth that much."

"I'll tell you what I'll do, Eddie—" Jules was grinning again "—I'll give you sixty just 'cause I like you." Jules stood up then. "Of course, we could make it an even hundred real easy." Jules reached down and patted the front of his pants.

Eddie slipped his hand in the front of his coat and took hold of the hatchet. "I'll just take the sixty . . . and my name isn't Eddie." He hoped the gesture would force Jules to back off.

Jules looked at Eddie for a long time. Finally, he moved his hand away from the front of his pants. He slowly reached into his pocket and took out three twenties. Then, even more slowly, he handed the money to Eddie. "Sometimes it doesn't pay to be unfriendly. It can come back to haunt you."

Eddie took the money with his left hand. His right hand was still holding the hatchet. He wasn't planning to let go of it until he was outside and on the street. He stuffed the money into a jacket pocket.

Jules sat back down. "Remember what I just told you, Eddie. Unfriendly things happen to unfriendly people."

Eddie was glad the man had sat down. Now there was room to get past him. Eddie turned sideways so he wouldn't have his back to Jules as he went by. Then he made his way to the door that separated the backroom from the rest of the place. Eddie wanted to say something. He wished he could think of the words that would wipe the grin off Jules's face. But he couldn't. Instead, he went through the first door, turned, and ran to the second.

Once he was outside, Eddie thought he was going to be sick. He bent over, put his hands on his knees and took several deep breaths. He'd read somewhere that breathing like that would keep you from getting sick. It seemed to work. His head felt clearer, and his stomach, at least for the moment, stopped doing somersaults.

Eddie jaywalked across to the other side of the street. He wanted to put some distance between himself and the creepy store with its even creepier guy inside.

He wanted to run. Not because he was scared. Jules hadn't scared him so much as made Eddie want to be somewhere else. Anywhere else. But Eddie didn't run. He knew that would be exactly the wrong thing to do—the kind of thing that got the cops' attention in a hurry. Especially around here.

One thing bothered Eddie. Jules knew his name—and what he looked like. That was bad, especially if the cops had been around to the store with Eddie's picture. Jules looked like the kind of guy who'd sell you out to the cops in a minute if there was a little profit in it. Plus, Jules was a pervert. Those guys were the worst mostly because you could never predict what they were going to do.

Eddie passed an antiques store, a health food restaurant, then a used-book store. At the corner he looked back up the street toward Eastside New and Used. There were a lot of people on the street, but he didn't see anything unusual.

Eddie tried to laugh. *Come on*, he told himself, *you're scarin' the crap out of yourself for nothing. Guys like Jules might like young boys, but they aren't going to jump you in broad daylight on a busy street.*

He was feeling better. He had sixty bucks in his pocket. Combined with what he got from the B and E, that would hold him for a while. And every step was taking him farther away from Jules. The street itself was okay. Actually, it was kind of neat. People were obviously trying to turn the once-dumpy area into something better. That was cool. There was a coffee shop a couple of places ahead. Eddie went inside. It was nice and cozy. Eddie laughed again as he thought about the job somebody was going to have trying to turn Eastside New and Used into a "nice and cozy" yuppie joint, too.

He sat down and ordered a coffee, then changed his mind and asked for it to go. He wanted to get back to the zoo. What was it his dad used to say? It didn't matter where you lived—it was always good to get home. The zoo was his home now and Eddie wanted to get back as fast as possible. He paid for the coffee, poured generous amounts of milk and sugar into the cardboard cup and went out onto the street. He turned right and walked as quickly as he dared in the direction of the zoo.

Seventeen

June 20, 2:45 P.M. There are horses at the zoo.
Not the kind you see in pastures in every direction
from Calgary. These horses are smaller. There
are only two of them and they look more like
early ancestors of the horse than like any
horse I've ever seen. The sign on the fence
outside their pen says they're Przewalski
horses—a wild breed that once lived in Mongolia
but are extinct there now. The remaining ones
live in zoos and on animal reserves.

Przewalski horses aren't pretty, but I don't
care. They're horses and that's good enough
for me. I've loved horses since I was a little
kid. I even had my own, this tall palomino named
Sonny. We kept him at a farm just on the edge
of Long Prairie. I spent a lot of time with him.
I even did my homework sitting on his back in
the paddock out behind the barn. Not that you
get a lot of homework in grades two and three,
but Sonny and me, we read a lot of picture
books together, too.

I liked these horses as soon as I saw them.
They're in an outdoor pen and now that the
weather is finally better, I'm over at that part
of the zoo a lot. There's this big boulder not far

from where they are, and I like sitting up there (that's where I am right now) writing stuff in my notebook or reading that mystery I ripped off in the B and E. Once in a while, for a treat, I bring along something from the snack bar. That's easier to do now that I've got a little cash.

Now that the B and E is over, I've been feeling . . . I guess you'd say relieved. And safer. I move around the zoo more now and I even sit here on this boulder in the middle of the day. I still get out of sight if I see zookeepers coming, but I don't hide when visitors are walking around. I figure it doesn't matter if someone who knows my mom or Steve sees me. Even if they mentioned that they'd seen me here, they'd probably think I'd been here for the day, like everybody else. Nobody is going to suspect I actually live in the place.

I've been trying to make friends with some of the animals. That part isn't going all that great. Except for the gorilla who seemed like she was reaching out to me, and the little duck that I see every morning, the animals pretty much ignore me. The Przewalski horses are no different.

Yesterday was a good day. I was sitting on the boulder and the weather was perfect. It seems like it's been windy every day since I've been here, but yesterday was totally still. And there was even a little bonus activity in the horse pen. The veterinarian and one of the zookeepers were trimming the horses' feet. Even with the weather as nice as it was, the zoo wasn't very busy and almost no one came along to watch the hoof-trimming ritual. I was kind of happy about that. It made it feel like this was my private place and these were my horses.

They had to tranquilize the horses ("tranked" I heard the veterinarian say), so they'd stand quietly while the work was being done. The zoo-keeper held one of the horses while the veterinarian worked. Even though they were tranked, the horses got impatient once in a while, and the zookeeper almost got run over a couple of times. The veterinarian worked quickly and carefully. The idea seemed to be to do a reasonable job without getting kicked while doing it, which made sense to me. First, he gave the horses another needle—probably just something to keep them healthy. We had to give needles to Sonny sometimes. Then the vet started on the feet. First, he snipped off the part of the hoof that had grown long. Then he filed the hoof smooth and round. I watched until one horse was finished and the other had one foot left to do.

Eddie stopped writing and looked at his watch. It was just after four o'clock, time to go. Eddie had something to do. He'd made up his mind about it a few days earlier and today was the day.

Eddie wanted to go home. Not actually go in the house, of course, just close enough to watch. And, more important, to try to see his mother. It was Friday and that was the one day Steve let her out of the house on her own. On Friday nights Eddie's mother went to bingo.

Before Steve, Eddie couldn't remember his mom ever playing bingo. And he still couldn't imagine her enjoying the smoke-filled, car lot–size rooms people gathered in to play a game he had tired of in about grade five. Maybe it was just the chance to get out of the house and away from Steve for a while that made bingo appealing to his mother. That he could understand.

Or maybe it was Steve's idea that she go to bingo. After all, if she won anything it would bring money to a household that could use all the extra cash it could get. Whatever the reason, Friday night was bingo night, and on this particular bingo night, Eddie would be behind the lilac bushes near the bus stop across the street from his house. He would be able to see his mother without her seeing him.

It wasn't that he missed her. He would never forgive her for bringing Steve into their lives and letting him do the things he had done. No, he didn't miss her. Besides, he'd only been gone for two months. But she *was* his

177

mother. And he had to know that she was all right. That she was at least safe.

The bus was crowded. Eddie had walked downtown and caught the number six bus that went by his house. His mother would take the same bus to get to the bingo hall. Eddie looked around at the other riders. He was a little nervous. He still didn't want to see anyone he knew. It wouldn't have been a disaster, he told himself. He'd simply get off at the next stop and work out a different way of getting to the house.

The house. Not "his" house or "our" house. He didn't think of it that way anymore. The people who lived there weren't strangers, but they didn't seem linked to him in any real way either. They didn't feel like family.

As he sat looking out the window, Eddie thought about his mother. He hadn't thought about her much—hadn't let himself think about her—since he'd left home. But now, with the diesel drone of the bus and the muffled conversation of the passengers as background, Eddie Slater let the thoughts creep in.

What had happened? The woman who lived in the house on Forty-fourth Avenue was so different from the person who had been his mom when he was growing up in Long Prairie. It was hard to believe she was the same person. How could that have happened? Did she love Steve so much that she was willing to stop being who she was? And had she been willing to abandon her child along the way?

Or had she just lost interest in her son—and life? That was what it seemed like to Eddie. Yet how was that possible? How could the woman who had been so interesting—and interested—when he was small have changed into the dull, lifeless person he knew now? He couldn't remember the last real conversation he and his mother had had.

Had they *ever* done that? Or was that something he'd just dreamed? Made up, somehow, out of hazy distant memories? No, he hadn't dreamed it. She *was* the smiling woman with the pickle-smelling hands on canning day. She *was* the person who sat on the edge of the bed when he was sick as a little boy. That was funny, too. His dad was there when he was scared and his mom was there when he was sick. Every time he woke up she was there, always with her soft voice and a touch that made even the mumps tolerable. She had been so special to him then and now she was . . . gone.

Was it fear that changed her? Eddie could have understood that, at least. No, that was wrong. He wouldn't have understood it, but at least he could have tolerated it . . . forgiven it. But could someone be so afraid of someone else that she would stand by while her child was being beaten senseless by a man who gave neither her nor that child one moment of happiness? How could that be?

He didn't know the answers. He wasn't even sure he was asking the right questions. But for the first time in a very long time, Eddie felt sorry for his mother. And he felt sad for what he had lost—what had been taken from him.

Eddie's eyes were wet. He turned farther toward the window to make sure no one could see. At least none of the tears were working their way down his cheek. If that happened he'd have to wipe them off and someone might notice. He opened his eyes as wide as they would go, partly to keep the tears in and partly to help them dry before they overflowed onto and then down his face.

Outside, the weather was changing. So much for the great day. Dark clouds were billowing up out of the north and moving fast toward the city. If they didn't veer off soon there would definitely be a storm. Maybe a bad one. *Not a great night to be out*, Eddie thought. But it didn't matter. This was something he wanted to do and he didn't want to wait another week.

He was mad at himself for almost crying. Just like the time he'd taken Patti Frederick to a movie and almost cried at the end. Jeez, how embarrassing had that been? And now here he was, in a standing-room-only bus, close to blubbering.

He wanted more than ever to see his mother. It crossed his mind that he might not. She might not go to bingo tonight. Steve might have stopped letting her out of the house at all. The sadness Eddie had been feeling gave way to anger. But it surprised him that it wasn't his mother he was angry at.

There were only a few people left on the bus by the time Eddie rang the bell. The stop he had chosen was four blocks from his house. He was the only person to get off. The wind was whipping up and the temperature was dropping fast. Eddie looked at the sky. There was no way this storm was going to miss Calgary.

And, as usual, he hadn't dressed for the weather. He told himself it wasn't really his fault. There was no way he could have known about the storm. It had been beautiful all morning and into the afternoon.

He glanced at his watch. She should be leaving the house in about fifteen minutes. He pulled his collar up around his neck, shoved his hands in his pockets and started walking.

The rain started when he was still a block from the bus stop his mother would use. By the time he was in position behind the bushes, it was coming down hard—and sideways, thanks to the driving wind. The lilac bushes didn't offer much protection. *Maybe she won't be going to bingo tonight even if she had planned to. I wouldn't be out in this if I had a choice.*

Eddie looked over at Mr. and Mrs. Hunt's house. No lights on. He hoped Mr. Hunt was doing okay. Eddie decided he wouldn't wait long. He'd give his mother one bus. If she didn't get on that one, he wasn't hanging around.

He was already soaked and shivering. But she did come out of the house. She waited until the last minute. In fact, Eddie almost ran into her. The bus was almost at the stop and there was no sign of his mom, so Eddie had stepped out from behind the bushes to wait. That's when he noticed her running toward the stop from the house. If she hadn't had her head down and an umbrella in front of her as she crossed the street, she'd have seen him. As it was, Eddie barely had time to get back behind the lilac bushes.

The umbrella was covering her face and head, and she got on the bus so quickly that Eddie got only a brief look. No way he could tell if she was all right. No way he could tell anything. About all he could see was that she was wet, although not nearly as wet as him.

As the bus pulled away, Eddie leaned out of the bushes hoping to get a glimpse of her as she took her seat. But she sat on the far side of the bus and it pulled away and out of sight without his seeing her again.

So far, the evening had been a write-off. Here he was standing across the street from his former home about to catch pneumonia and he hadn't really done what he'd set out to do in the first place. Oh, he'd seen her all right, but he had no idea how she was doing. Of course, maybe he wouldn't have been able to tell that even if he *had* gotten a better look. Still, he would have liked that chance. And, to top it all off, he would now have to stand in the rain until the next bus came by. He could die first. *With my luck, the next bus will be a convertible.*

He didn't die. In fact, his luck improved. The next bus came along about five minutes later. Eddie had never been so glad to be inside something in his life.

The bus driver grinned at him. "Rotten night out there," he said as Eddie dropped his fare into the box.

"Yeah." Eddie nodded and tried to wipe some of the water from his face. The effort was wasted—his sleeve was at least as wet as his face.

The driver reached down, pulled a towel from a sports bag on the floor near his feet and handed it to Eddie. "I'm going to the gym later, but I think you need this more right now than I will then."

Eddie took the towel but hesitated. "Are you sure? How're you going to dry off after your shower?"

The driver waved a hand at Eddie as he eased the bus out into traffic. "I'll get one there. They got lots. Go ahead."

Eddie didn't argue further. He dried his face and hair, then handed the towel back to the driver. "Thanks . . . thanks a lot."

"Four seats back is a good place to sit. There's heat there. Should warm you up."

"Okay, thanks," Eddie said again. "If they ever have one of those Bus Driver of the Year awards, I'll put your name in."

The driver laughed. "They don't have one, and if they did, the prize would probably be a bus trip somewhere. Don't bother!"

Eddie started down the aisle of the bus, then stopped and turned back to the driver. "There's a big bingo place around here somewhere. You know where it is?"

"Sure, it's up a ways. I go pretty close to it. You want, I can let you know when we get to that stop."

"Yeah, please, that'd be great."

Eddie counted back four seats and sat down. The driver was right. Heat was pumping out of a big vent down by his feet. It wasn't long before Eddie was feeling warm and even a little drier.

He had a decision to make. He wasn't sure why he had asked the driver about the bingo place. He couldn't go in and risk being seen by his mother. And he sure as hell wasn't planning to stand around outside until she left. So what difference did it make whether he knew where it was or not? But now that he'd asked, he'd look pretty stupid if he didn't get off at that stop. "I hope there's a coffee shop somewhere close by," he whispered to the rain that was pounding against the bus's window.

Eddie was still thinking about what to do when the driver cranked his head around and looked at him. "Next stop for D.J.'s Bingo Palace. They tell me D.J. is pretty much a crook, so don't plan to win much."

"How can you cheat at bingo?" Eddie stood up and walked to the front of the bus.

"If there's a way, D.J. will find it." The driver braked the bus to a stop and opened the front door. "It's just around this corner and half a block up. If you run like hell, you might not get too wet."

"Right," Eddie said as he stepped off the bus and onto the sidewalk. There was no sign of a coffee shop anywhere. The rain had eased a little, but Eddie knew he'd soon be soaked again if he didn't take the driver's advice.

He ran. And as he did he formulated a plan. He'd go into the bingo hall. The place was huge, he knew that much. If he could spot his mother before she saw him, he'd be able to find a safe place to watch her. As he got closer to D.J.'s, with its gaudy neon sign telling the world there was a twenty-five-hundred-dollar blackout bonus winner every Friday night, Eddie could see holes in his plan. Quite a few holes.

First of all, there was a good chance that his mother *would* see him, maybe even as he was walking in the door. Or, if she didn't, someone who knew them both might spot him and tell her he was there. And even if neither of those things happened, there was still one critical flaw in his plan. What was he going to *do* in there? He couldn't just lean against the wall the way he did at school dances. What did people do in a bingo place but play bingo? And Eddie wasn't about to play bingo.

He was relieved to see a lineup of people going in the front door. That was good. He'd be able to lose himself in the crowd and at least be able to get in the building without being seen.

Eddie worked himself in behind a couple of older women. They turned and looked at him, then at each other, but didn't say anything. The line moved quickly and Eddie found himself inside the door and at a table. Three people, a man and two women, were at the table taking money and handing out cards.

Eddie stopped in front of the man.

"How many, Peewee?"

Peewee. Eddie stared blankly at the man. "How many what?"

"Cards, bingo cards, that's what we do here."

"Uh . . . one."

Eddie heard someone laugh.

"They come in sixes," the man behind the table said.

"Really?" Eddie looked around. Each card was the size of a poster turned on its side and contained six cards, three along the top and three along the bottom. Everybody had at least two of the large cards. Some had three, meaning they would somehow keep track of eighteen bingo cards at once. "How much for six?"

"You picked a good night to come, Peewee. It's five-buck night. You get six cards and a dauber for five bucks."

Eddie got a five-dollar bill out of his pocket and handed it to the man. "What do you do with a dauber?" Eddie heard laughter again.

"What the hell do you think you do with a dauber? You daub, that's what. You take the dauber and when the caller calls a number that's on your cards, you take the dauber . . . and . . . you . . . daub . . . on the numbers. You with me on that, Peewee?"

Eddie placed his hands palms down on the table and leaned forward so that his face was very close to the man's. "Are you D.J. by any chance?"

The man grinned. "Heard of me, huh?"

"I've heard of you," Eddie said in a low voice. "And if you call me Peewee again, I'll take that dauber . . . and . . . shove . . . it . . . up your ass. You with me on that, D.J.?"

The laughing behind Eddie stopped. D.J. stood up. He was a little taller and a lot wider than Eddie. He looked at Eddie for a long time, until Eddie was sure the man was about to grab him and throw him out of the hall. He was wrong. D.J. sat back down and looked past Eddie at the people behind him.

"Let's get it movin'," he growled. "First game starts in five minutes."

Eddie picked up his cards and dauber and turned into the bingo hall. He tried to stay tucked in behind the other people who were moving into the hall, while still scouring the room for his mother.

He was in luck. She was at a row of tables on the far right. Her back was to him. Eddie worked his way down the left side of the room and found a spot at a table that allowed him to watch his mother. He sat down and set his cards on the table in front of him.

Two women sat across from him. They had five of the big cards spread out in front of them. The woman on the left was big, real big. She was smoking and eating french fries at the same time. The woman on the right had hair so red it looked fake, not just dyed but more like a wig or something. Both women smiled at him. The big woman needed dental work in a major way. *Maybe she was Stink Pagler's mother.* Red Hair's teeth were okay, but her painted-on eyebrows looked as fake as her hair. *Maybe she drew them with crayon*, Eddie speculated as he smiled back.

"First time, Cutes?" Red Hair asked.

"Uh . . . yeah." Eddie nodded. *Cutes? That's even worse than Peewee.*

"A virgin bingo player. Ain't that just too damn sweet for words?" Big Woman grinned. Eddie hoped she wouldn't do that anymore.

"You know what to do?" Red Hair asked him.

"Not exactly," Eddie admitted. "I guess you're supposed to daub."

"Yeah, but only the numbers you need to win the game. You get what I'm saying?"

Eddie shook his head. "Nope."

"Okay, let's say we're playing an L game. That's where you need all the numbers under the B but only the bottom numbers under all the other letters. So it looks like an L."

Big Woman stuck another french fry in her mouth and pointed at one of Eddie's cards. "See that N–36. It's at

188

the top of the row, so it won't help you make an L. Don't daub that one."

"Makes sense." Eddie nodded. "Thanks."

"Of course, for the blackout, you fill 'em all in. You win that one, Cutes, and I'll take you home with me."

Red Hair was about to explain more of the game's fine points when the caller yelled "Check One-Two" into the microphone.

"Too loud . . . turn it down, Al," a chorus of voices protested.

Al turned it down. "All right, everybody . . . LET'S GET READY TO RUM . . . BLE!"

Eddie stifled a grin. The guy couldn't be serious. Surely he wasn't thinking he could make an EVENT out of a bingo game. This night was going to be an education if nothing else. And it might even be fun. Across the table, Big Woman and Red Hair had suddenly turned serious. Daubers poised, they scanned their cards even before the first number was called. Were they trying to memorize the cards, or impart some good-luck spell onto the numbers? Eddie wasn't sure.

He looked around. The majority of the players were women. And most looked pretty normal . . . ordinary. Eddie had always figured that the people who frequented these places were likely to be on the weird side. Big Woman and Red Hair had done nothing to change that opinion. But now, as he looked around the room, he was surprised to see people who looked like they could be wives, mothers, grandmothers, business people, maybe even professional women—regular people. There were men scattered here and there as well, but they weren't nearly as interesting as the women. One thing all of them had in common—they all looked pretty intense when it came to playing bingo.

Eddie could see his mother if he leaned a little to his right. It was only her back, but he was surprised at the feeling it gave him to be this close to her. It felt good to have her just across the room and it bugged him a little that he felt that way.

"First game will be a cross," Al announced over the microphone.

"Shit," Big Woman said without taking her eyes off the cards. "I never win the cross."

"Daub your free ones."

Eddie didn't move.

"Daub your free ones." It was Red Hair who was speaking and Eddie realized the advice was for him. "It's bad luck not to," she added.

"Okay." He daubed the free centre square on all six cards.

"The cross goes down the middle and across the middle."

"Right," Eddie said.

"Eyes down," Al directed over the microphone.

That suggestion was totally unnecessary. As Eddie looked around the room, it was clear that the only eyes not facing down were his own.

"This is a gas." He hadn't realized he'd said it out loud until Red Hair let her eyes flick up at him for about a nanosecond.

"Better be ready," she warned. "It happens pretty fast."

"Under the N . . . three and six . . . thirty-six," Al announced.

Eddie wondered what the "three and six" was all about. Why didn't he just say, "Under the N . . . thirty-six?" *Showbiz*, Eddie decided.

Eddie had N–36 on three of his cards. He daubed all three. "Yeah!" he said to no one in particular. It was a good start. But he didn't win the cross game. Nor did he win the postage stamp game or the L game. In fact, he wasn't even close. But he didn't mind losing; it was fun to be with people again. After each game he looked across the room at his mother. When the postage stamp game ended, she went to the concession, bought a coffee and took it back to her table. Two creams and one sugar, Eddie remembered.

Al informed them that the next game was an X. By this time Eddie didn't need any explanation from his coaches across the table. The game started and suddenly his luck seemed to change. Two of the cards in particular kept him busy and suddenly he needed only one number on one of the cards, G–57. Al called one number, B–9, then another, O-Clickety-Click-66 and then I–21. A woman a couple of tables away called bingo.

"Damn." Eddie smacked his dauber on the table. "What's he got against G–57 anyway?"

"Hello, Eddie."

For a second Eddie didn't recognize the voice. When he did, he raised his head slowly. His mother was standing between and just behind Big Woman and Red Hair. She didn't seem mad or even surprised.

"Uh . . . hi."

She looked smaller somehow, though Eddie knew that didn't make sense. Mostly she looked . . . the same. Short, dark hair around a face shaped kind of like a heart. It was a soft face with pale green eyes—the same face that he remembered looking so intensely at him on those nights when he'd been sick and she'd sit beside him. A thought crossed Eddie's mind; one that he couldn't remember ever having before. His mother was pretty. She was wearing a soft yellow sweater and pants that looked like jeans but weren't denim.

She was smiling, but that part wasn't the same. Eddie had loved his mother's smile when he was little, especially the way her eyes sort of lit up. He hadn't seen that smile in a long time and he wasn't seeing it now. The corners of her mouth turned, up but her eyes remained flat, lifeless.

She was twisting a napkin in her hands. She looked more nervous than anything. "I . . . had it all worked out in my mind what I was going to say when . . . if . . . I saw you again, but I can't remember any of it."

Red Hair looked at Big Woman. "There's a break before the next game. I think we should get some coffee."

The women stood up. As she went past Eddie's mother, Red Hair put a thick hand on the smaller woman's arm. "You take my chair right there, honey. And you take as long as you want, I wasn't winning anything with those stinking cards anyway."

Eddie's mother sat down. For a long time she didn't say anything, and when she did finally speak her voice seemed unsure. "Are you doing okay?"

"Yeah." Eddie nodded. "I'm doing okay."

"Good." The napkin broke from the twisting and Eddie's mother set the two halves down on the table. She took a deep breath, then another. "Steve's gone."

Eddie didn't move. He wasn't sure what he had expected his mother to say, but that wasn't it. "You throw him out?"

Eddie's mother shook her head. "He walked out on me. A month ago. Went to Vancouver with someone he met line dancing. She . . . she was twenty."

"Years old?" Eddie almost laughed. The big line dancer had run off with a girl only five years older than Eddie. That was one of the funniest things he'd heard in a long time. It was bloody hilarious. A crazy thought slipped into Eddie's mind. *Maybe they don't line dance in Vancouver.* That would be the funniest thing of all.

But he didn't laugh. He leaned back in his chair and looked at his mother. "You never would've told him to leave, would you?"

"I . . . don't know. I never got the chance."

"Never got the chance," Eddie repeated, shaking his head. "You had a million chances. What you never got was the jam."

Eddie's mother opened her mouth then shut it without saying anything. She looked down at her hands.

Eddie felt the old anger building up inside him. "You would've let that wacko stay forever, even if he killed me. He broke up our family and you chose him. You chose him over and over. Why was that, Mom?" He drew out the word "Mom" to make it sound like something bad.

"Why don't you come back home, Eddie? I want you to come back home."

"Yeah? Right up until he comes back. Then you won't give a damn if I'm there or not. Then I'll be Eddie the punching bag again until I either run away or end up on life-support. I don't think so." Eddie could feel himself getting louder, but he couldn't help it. He'd been angry for too long.

"He won't be coming back," his mother said. "Steve won't be back."

"How do you know that?" Eddie leaned forward, his forearms on the table. "You didn't throw him out. He left you for a . . . for someone younger. What happens when he gets tired of her? You'll just open that door and—"

"I tried once."

"What?"

"I tried to get him to leave once. It was after he'd beaten you up for something, I don't remember what. I told him I was calling the police. He said if I did, he'd kill us both. I didn't care what he did to me, but I was afraid . . . I . . . he would have done it, Eddie, I know that."

"He almost killed me anyway."

"I know."

"So after I was gone, why didn't you get rid of him then?"

"I hoped you might come back. I thought if I could just make him happy somehow, that maybe he'd leave you alone and we could be—"

"Happy?" Eddie interrupted. "Did you honestly think we could ever actually be happy with that psycho in our house? You know how you said that you couldn't remember what he'd been beating on me for the time you almost called the police? Well, guess what, Mom? I can remember what it was for *every* time." He pointed to a mark on his arm, one that hadn't completely healed. "That one? I got that for dropping a book on the floor when he was watching TV. 'Too noisy,' he said. I've got this nice scar on my back. That was for walking too slow when I was bringing him a cup of coffee. And there's—"

"Please don't do this, Eddie." There were tears in his mother's eyes.

Eddie could feel his own tears forcing their way out. "What do you want me to say? You want me to say, 'Don't worry about it, Mom. It's okay.' Well, it's not okay. It's not okay, Mom."

She nodded, then picked up one of the twisted halves of the napkin and wiped her eyes. "Why did you come here tonight?" she asked.

195

"Because . . . because I wanted to see you. Weird, eh? I wanted to know if you were all right."

"Eddie . . . why don't you think about coming home?"

Eddie stood up. "I don't want to come home. I like being by myself. I think I'll just keep things that way for a while."

"Somebody said it's still raining outside. Maybe you should come home just for tonight."

"I've got a good place to stay. I'll be fine . . . thanks anyway." He meant it. He appreciated the offer, but this wasn't the right time. He wasn't sure if there would ever be a right time. He wondered if his mother could see that in his face.

She reached across the table. "Well, take this at least." It was a twenty-dollar bill.

"I'm okay . . . really."

"Please take it. Maybe you can get yourself some veal cutlets or something. I know how much you like veal cutlets."

He took the money and shoved it in a pocket. "Thanks." He stood up, took a couple of steps up the aisle then turned back to her. "I'll think about what you said."

Eddie walked quickly out of the bingo hall. He was glad it was still raining. No one would be able to tell that some of the wet on his cheeks had nothing to do with rain.

Eighteen

The bus stop had a shelter and he squeezed inside with several other people. The rain was pouring down harder again, but with the wind coming from behind the shelter not much of it was getting in.

"Some rain, huh?" somebody said. Eddie didn't look around to see if the speaker was talking to him. He didn't feel like talking.

"I heard it's supposed to do this most of the night," a second person said.

"You'd think we were in Vancouver," the first voice replied.

Eddie was glad when the lights of the bus appeared down the street. He moved out of the shelter to wait at the curb even though it meant standing in the rain. He wanted more than anything to be by himself. He wanted to think, and how hard it would rain and for how long was the last thing he wanted to think about.

He got on the bus and was glad when nobody sat beside him. He stared straight ahead, not seeing anything but the pictures in his head. They weren't nice pictures. He could see Steve's face, twisted with uncontrollable fury; his fist coming down, again and again. And sometimes even that wasn't enough to satisfy Steve's need to hurt. Then it was weapons, whatever he could lay his hands on. A hockey stick, a beer bottle, the massive belt buckle and finally the cord from the iron, each one with its own set of marks left behind. But there was always the pain. Eddie could count on that every time.

Now Steve was gone. What did that change? Anything? Eddie believed his mother when she said Steve had threatened to kill them both. But surely when she'd been down the hall and heard his screams . . . that's when she should have done something. And she hadn't.

That was the worst picture of all: the picture of his mother sitting—maybe with her hands over her ears to keep out the sound of his pain—*letting it happen.*

Eddie almost missed his stop. He wasn't paying attention and the bus was about to pull away when he realized that this was where he had to transfer to the bus that would go by the zoo. Eddie jumped up and rang the bell. He pulled the cord three or four times. The driver stopped and looked back.

"Take it easy. I can hear the bell whether you pull it once or fifty times."

Another time Eddie might have smart-mouthed the driver, but this time he just shrugged and mumbled "Sorry" as he quickly stepped off. If anything, the rain was coming down even harder now. Eddie was glad to see another bus shelter and he hurried inside. He thought ahead to the run from the bus stop to the condo. He wasn't looking forward to it, but he could hardly wait to be in under the rock outcrop, dry and far away from the whole world. The bus came and Eddie was its only passenger. He was glad. *No more stupid conversation.*

This time Eddie was ready for his stop. From the moment he'd stepped onto the bus, he hadn't stopped looking out into the wild blustering night. When the doors hissed open, he hit the pavement running. He calculated as he ran. Two long blocks or maybe three short ones, then down the fence to the hole. A short sprint past Dinny to the stream. Over the fence and to the condo. He'd pull his clothes off outside; it would be too hard to get the wet stuff off in the tiny space.

Lightning cracked off to his right and a few seconds later an explosion of thunder made him flinch. He was at the fence. Climbing through the hole he snagged his shirt. Now it was both sopping wet *and* ruined. *Damn . . . trying to hurry too much.*

He forced himself to slow down. More lightning and another clap of thunder, not as loud this time. As he worked himself free, he realized he was out of breath from the run. There was no point in sprinting anymore. He couldn't possible get any wetter. He trotted easily away from the fence and toward Dinny.

Even without thunder the noise of the storm was so loud he could barely hear the slap of his runners on the wet pavement. Water was running down his face and into his eyes and it wasn't easy to see.

Maybe that's why he didn't see them. Not until he practically ran into them. He would have been surprised to see two people out anywhere on a night like this, but especially here. It looked as if they had been standing under

Dinny's huge belly. He hoped it was just a couple of visitors who hadn't gotten out before closing time. Better that than security guards.

But it wasn't visitors or security guards. For the second time that night, Eddie was surprised by a voice he hadn't expected to hear.

"It's been a long time, Eddie. Nice to catch up with you again."

. Another flash of lightning, this one right overhead, seemed to light up the whole world.

Stink Pagler was grinning. In that first stab of panic Eddie didn't recognize the other man right away. He was grinning, too. And Eddie had seen that grin before. As the lightning lingered a second longer, Eddie remembered where he'd seen it.

Jules didn't say anything, he just grinned and let Stink do the talking.

"Kind of a good night to die, don't you think, Eddie?" Stink Pagler took a step forward.

Eddie stepped back. As he did he heard a click and looked down to see a switchblade in Stink Pagler's hand. Eddie knew that Stink wasn't kidding and wasn't just trying to scare him. Stink would cut him up bad and enjoy the experience. And he had a feeling that Jules wasn't just along to watch. Stink would probably get a charge out of letting Jules have some fun with Eddie before it was all over.

It was a bad dream. This stuff only happened on TV and in the movies. The thought kept flashing like a neon sign in Eddie's head. *Bad dream. Bad dream.* Eddie hoped he'd wake up soon.

But it wasn't a bad dream. It was real, and as lightning flashed again, this time farther to the west, the pair took another step closer toward Eddie.

Eddie wanted to run, but he couldn't. It was like the fear that had taken over his mind had willed his body to stay frozen in place. Yelling was useless. The storm had no doubt driven the security guards indoors, and even if they were out on the grounds, they'd have to be standing almost next to Eddie to hear him over the roar of the storm.

"How . . . how did you know I was here?" It didn't really matter and he didn't think they'd bother to answer him, but he needed time to think. If he could keep them talking even for a minute or two maybe he could come up with an idea.

"Well, you see, Eddie—" Stink studied the blade of the knife as he spoke "—I asked around and some people told me you like to break into houses. Now, that surprised me. I never would've thought a little puke like you would have the guts. Guess I was wrong. Guess you must be a tough guy after all. And tonight we're gonna find out how tough you are." Stink spat on the pavement.

"Anyway, I figured you might need to fence some stuff sometime so I stopped by and talked to my friend Jules. I said if a skinny dumb-shit kid came in to the store that he should maybe find out where the skinny dumb-shit kid went and let me know. So when you left Jules's little business palace, he just followed you back here."

Eddie looked at Jules. The man was so puffed up with Pagler's praise that he looked as if he could explode at any minute. Weird that a guy Jules's age would think that a teenager was some kind of hero. But then again, Jules *was* weird.

"I told you ya should've been a little friendlier." Jules put his hand on the front of his pants, just like he had that day in the store. "But maybe we can do something about that unfriendly attitude of yours."

"We got a place picked out for our little meeting," Stink said, "so let's get out of the rain and let the games begin." Stink laughed at that. The laugh was high-pitched, not what Eddie expected at all.

Eddie backed up again, but he was running out of room. There was a temporary fence behind him. He remembered the workmen putting it up a few days before. What the hell had they put a fence here for anyway?

He was out of room and would soon be out of options. He couldn't go forward or backward. Stink was on his left, and the switchblade he was brandishing made that option very unappealing. That left only the right.

A clap of thunder roared overhead, the loudest one so far. All three jumped at the ear-splitting crash. Eddie used the temporary distraction to make his move. He bolted to his right and past Jules before the older man could react.

Eddie wasn't much of an athlete, but he had always been fast. And desperate fear was a powerful motivator. He had never been more scared in his life—not even with Steve. He was closer than he'd ever been to his own death and he knew that these two creeps would make it as horrible as they could.

He ran hard. But the sprint from the bus had tired him out, and he wasn't sure how long he could keep it up. He managed a peek over his shoulder. When it came to running, Stink was no slouch. He wasn't far back and Eddie hadn't been able to put any more distance between them. He couldn't see Jules, but it didn't matter. He knew that when the bad stuff started Jules would be there.

It was dark. Some of the zoo's night lights were off, probably knocked out by the storm. Eddie ran on instinct. He didn't know exactly where he was and he had no plan. He just knew that he had to keep running.

If only he could see. But between the dark and the blinding rain he couldn't make out much more than vague shapes. He was afraid he might run into something. That would be fatal.

He chanced another look over his shoulder. Stink was farther back now and it looked as if he was having as much trouble seeing as Eddie was. Stink was fast, but he wasn't in real good shape, Eddie could see that. As tough as Stink was, long-distance running required stamina that he didn't have. Maybe there was a chance for Eddie after all.

Eddie was running on a paved walkway. Now it branched both left and right, and he went left. But as he made the sharp turn, his feet went out from under him, bringing him down hard. He tried to bounce back up, but pain exploded where his right kneecap had made contact with the pavement.

Eddie forced himself to get up. The pain was terrible and each limping stride seemed to make it worse. He knew he couldn't go much farther. He stared hard into the rain. There had to be something out there that might give him a chance.

There. Over there to the left. A structure, vaguely familiar. Desperately Eddie made for it.

It was the wrong thing to do. What he'd seen was Last Sam's cage and not until he was through its open door did he remember that there was only one way in and out.

He turned around quickly. This was no good. He had to get out. He had to run somewhere . . . anywhere. He took one painful step toward the cage's door and stopped. Stink Pagler was blocking the way. He was slumped forward, gasping, with his hands on his knees, but he was looking up at Eddie and still grinning.

Eddie knew he was beaten, but he was too tired and too sore to care. He hoped only that whatever was going to happen would happen quickly. The terrible answer to that thought came as Jules stumbled into the cage behind Stink.

For a long minute no one spoke. Aside from the rain, the only sound was their breathing, each hungrily gulping at the damp air. Eddie stood on one leg—he could put almost no weight on the injured one—and looked around. There would be no escape.

The thunder and lightning had moved off, farther away now. And suddenly the rain began to let up. Too late to do him any good. Eddie's mind was working fast, but his thoughts were disjointed. *Think, think!* He couldn't seem to make his brain work right.

Weird. All those times I thought Steve would kill me and I end up getting a knife in the guts when he isn't even in the picture anymore.

As Stink moved toward him, Eddie backed up. A couple of shuffle steps and his back was against the bars of the cage. Stink came closer now and held the knife out at Eddie's eye level. Stink Pagler was going to take his time. He was going to enjoy getting his revenge.

Eddie tried to think of something . . . anything to say. He thought about begging, wondering if that might save him. But he knew it wouldn't, that it would only add to Stink's enjoyment. No, he wouldn't beg.

"You should think about getting some dental work. You are one ugly bast—"

He didn't get to finish the sentence. Stink kicked him in the stomach and Eddie folded up on the ground, new waves of pain rolling over and over him. The kick had propelled the air out of him like he was a popped balloon and he could hear himself making sucking sounds as he tried to get new air.

"You were pretty good at kicking the last time—" Stink's voice seemed to be far away "—it don't look like you enjoy it quite as much when you're the one getting kicked."

Eddie didn't see the second kick coming. It caught him in the ribs. He heard a crack and knew that something inside him had broken. He braced himself for the next blow, but his face was against the floor of the cage and he couldn't see Stink. He tried to get up, but the pain was too great. He felt himself sinking into a thick, black fog.

As he slipped in and out of consciousness, he was dimly aware of the nasal whine of Jules's voice. "Hey, man, don't forget what you promised. You're gonna kill the little bastard before I get to teach him how to be real friendly."

Eddie felt Stink take hold of his hair. He was being pulled to his feet. He groaned. The pain was awful and he could taste blood in his mouth. He was on his knees with Stink standing over him. Eddie tried to get his good leg underneath him. He could feel Jules groping at his belt.

"Let's get those pants off, little man," Jules's voice was singsong and disgusting. Eddie wanted to block it out, but he couldn't. Stink jerked him to his feet and Eddie groaned again. The black fog seemed to be inviting him in again. Eddie felt himself slipping . . . slipping . . .

Suddenly, the world exploded around him. This wasn't unconsciousness, he knew that. It was something else. He tried to figure it out, make sense of it, but he couldn't.

There was a shape. Moving fast. What was it? Then a noise, a loud noise, like a roar. Was it Last Sam? Did he want his cage back?

Eddie had fallen back down and was on his side now. Nobody was pulling his hair or kicking him. He tried to push his way through the fog, to open his eyes. He wanted to see what had made the roar.

He forced his eyes open. But what he saw didn't make any sense. Jack Simm, here . . . now. That didn't figure at all. Eddie could see Jules lying on his back with a lot of blood on his face. He wasn't moving. And there was Jack, kneeling over Stink. Jack had a knife. It wasn't the switch-blade. This was a big knife—the knife Eddie had seen in Jack's house.

He forced himself up on one elbow. He had to know if this was real, that it wasn't part of the fog-dream. Jack was holding the knife up to Stink Pagler's face. Jack's other hand had one of Stink's arms twisted around behind his back.

"You're a dead man, you goddamn psycho," Stink screamed, then spat in Jack's face.

Now that the storm had ended, there was a heavy silence all around. The only sounds that broke the stillness were the ones Jack and Stink were making. Jack made a small movement. There was a crack and Stink screamed. Eddie knew that Jack had broken Stink's arm.

Stink's scream died out and was replaced by a moan.

"Now here's the deal, boy—" Jack hissed the words into Stink's face.

"You can stick your deal up your ass, old man." Stink's face was twisted with pain and rage.

"You're not listening," Jack said quietly. He flicked his wrist, a movement so small and so quick that Eddie barely saw it. But now there was blood streaming out of a cut next to Stink Pagler's nose. "Are you ready to listen now?"

"You son of a—"

Jack's hand moved again and there was another cut, this one at the corner of Stink's eye. "I should probably tell you I'm pretty good with this thing. I can flick your eye out just as easy as I can cut alongside it. So maybe you should think about listening to what I have to say."

Stink's eyes were wide open now. He seemed to grasp that whoever this man was, he was dangerous. He opened his mouth, then closed it.

"Good." Jack's voice was soft as death. Though he couldn't see Jack's face, Eddie knew that all the guilt and fury and hate that Jack had carried inside him since that day so many years before was coming out now. Eddie wondered if Stink Pagler realized how close he was to dying.

"This boy is my friend," he heard Jack's voice telling Stink. "I don't want anything to happen to him. Not tonight. Not ever. And if anything does happen to him, anything—and that includes your sick friend over there—I'm going to assume that you're the one responsible. I'll find you and I'll finish renovating your face. And when I'm finished, your mother won't recognize you. Do you understand what I'm telling you?"

"Yeah."

"Good. Understand this as well—" Jack used the point of the knife to turn Stink's face so that Stink was looking at him "—it's all I can do to keep from killing you tonight. I can't tell you how much I want to leave you right here on the floor of this cage. Either one of you give me a reason—ever—and there isn't a thing in this world that will stop me from doing that. Nothing in this world."

"Nothing . . . will happen . . . to him," Stink Pagler's voice signalled his surrender.

Eddie knew Stink meant it. He knew he would never have to fear Stink or his crowd ever again. It was all there in the five words he'd just spoken. Not the words themselves, but the way he'd said them.

Without moving the tip of the knife from Stink's cheek, Jack looked over his shoulder at Eddie. In that instant Eddie understood why Stink had made the promise. In his whole life, Eddie had never seen anything like the look on Jack's face. It was the look of suffering and fear and hate and death. It was like looking at the end of the world. Eddie hoped he would never see anything like it ever again.

Eddie moved. He wanted to get up. But as he moved, the pain surrounded him again and the black fog rolled around and over him. The fog was thicker now and it felt warm, inviting. Eddie let himself drift into the soft, welcoming folds of the misty darkness.

Nineteen

When Eddie woke up, he was lying in the same position as when he'd passed out. But it was different now. He was in a bed, a clean bed with white sheets and pillowcases. In fact, the whole place was clean.

He tried to roll over, but it hurt too much. He moved his eyes as far as they would go to the left and then to the right, but all he got was floor in one direction and ceiling in the other.

"I see you've decided to join us," a pleasant female voice said. The voice came from behind him.

Eddie knew where he was now, or at least he thought he did. "Is this a hospital?"

"Clinic," came the answer from the same voice. "Like a hospital only smaller. How are you feeling?"

"Okay," Eddie said. "How did I get here?"

"Your dad brought you."

"Where is he . . . my dad?" Eddie's throat hurt to talk. He wasn't sure why that was. He didn't remember getting kicked or punched anywhere around his neck. Maybe on top of everything else he was getting a cold. He almost smiled at the thought.

"I'm here, kid, right here." Jack came around in front of Eddie and sat down on a chair next to the window.

Eddie remembered it all. Right up until the moment he passed out, he could recall perfectly every detail. But what had happened after that? He wanted to ask Jack, but he didn't think it was a good time with the nurse, if that's what she was, in the room.

"It's daylight," Eddie said. "I must have been out a long time."

Jack smiled at him. "You missed all of last night and most of today."

"How soon can I get out of here?"

"You've got a couple of cracked ribs, your knee is swelled up like a pumpkin and you've got some bumps and bruises. They tell me we should be able to get you out of here in a couple of days. They need to make sure there isn't any other damage to your insides first."

The woman's voice spoke again. "If you don't need anything right now, I'll leave you two to talk. But not too long. The more rest he gets, the quicker he'll recover."

Eddie waited until he heard the sound of the woman's footsteps fading before he turned his eyes to look at Jack. "What were you doing there . . . at Last Sam's cage?"

Jack looked down at his hands. "It doesn't matter. Why don't we just forget about it."

Eddie shook his head. "No. It does matter. I want to know."

Jack looked at him, nodded a little nod. "I'd seen that guy, not the one you call Stink—the other one—following you a while back. He did a pretty good job of staying out of sight, but I happened to spot him. He followed you until you got to Dinny, then he left. I thought about going after him then, but I didn't. Guess I should've."

Eddie watched Jack's eyes. They were soft now, so different from what Eddie had seen only hours before.

"The more I thought about it," Jack went on, "the more I thought he might be out to cause you some grief. He looked like the type that might want to do that. I decided I'd better see if I could prevent that from happening. So I've been watching you ever since he followed you. Just at night. I didn't figure he'd try anything during the day."

"You were at the playground all day and then you watched over me at night."

"Something like that, yeah." There was no emotion in Jack's voice. It was as if all the emotion had been spent in Last Sam's cage. Jack had saved Eddie's life, but he talked about it now like he was describing a drive in the country. Eddie knew there was no point in asking what had happened after he passed out. Jack Simm wouldn't say. And maybe that was better.

"Didn't you have to fill out forms? To get me in here?"

"Yeah, that's when I told them you were my kid. I figured that might be the best way to go. You didn't have any ID on you so nobody knows any different so far. I don't know how long we're going to get by without a health card, but so far so good."

"How do they think I got like this?" Eddie asked. He knew that there would probably be some suspicion that Jack had hurt him.

"I told them you were in a fight. Got jumped by two punks. Some kind of school feud."

Eddie nodded. Not a bad story. Part of it was even true. "Have you told anybody else I'm here?"

Jack leaned back in the chair. "I figure it's up to you to let your mother know what's going on . . . when you're ready."

Eddie didn't say anything. He didn't have an answer to that. At least not yet.

"You want anything? Water or anything?" Jack asked him.

Eddie tried to look at his watch, but it was gone. "The time," he said.

"What?" Jack turned his eyes back to Eddie.

"What time is it?"

Jack looked at his watch. "A little after three o'clock."

"Can you help me turn over on my back?" Eddie asked. "I'm getting stiff and I don't think I can roll over by myself."

"Sure, kid." Jack stood up and eased an arm behind Eddie's back. "Okay, I've got you. Now, nice and slow."

The turn wasn't that bad. It hadn't hurt as much as Eddie had thought it would. Jack straightened up and stood beside Eddie's bed. Eddie turned his head to look at him. "Three o'clock," he repeated.

"Yeah, maybe a few minutes after."

"How come you're not at the playground? You're always there at this time. The zoo doesn't close for another couple of hours."

Jack took a long time to answer. When he did, the beginning of a smile played at the corners of his mouth. "I guess I won't be doing that anymore."

"You won't be watching the kids at the playground anymore?"

"No." The smile got a little bigger. It wasn't a grin—Eddie couldn't imagine that face ever grinning—but for Jack Simm it was a pretty major smile.

Jack brushed an imaginary crumb off his shirt. "I don't have to do that anymore. I mean, it's not like I evened the score—nothing could do that. But I . . . I always said if only I could save one kid from something like what happened to Angela, maybe I could . . ." His voice broke as he said his sister's name and he brushed again at the front of his shirt.

"Yeah," Eddie said.

For several minutes neither of them spoke. Eddie stared up at the ceiling. "You think you'll ever go back there, to the zoo I mean?"

"I don't think so." Jack's voice was okay again. "I think it's time I saw a few other things in the world. How about you?"

Eddie tried to take a deep breath, but his ribs hurt too much. He took a couple of little breaths instead. "When I was in that cage and Stink Pagler was kicking me and I was sure I was going to die, right in the middle of the pain and everything I had this one thought. I remember thinking, just for a second, that the crappy part about dying right then was not ever going home again. I think maybe once I'm healed up and stuff I might, you know . . . just go home."

Jack Simm put his hand on Eddie's arm. "I think that's a pretty good idea."

Twenty

Jack Simm did go back to the zoo. Just once. He and Eddie went together. It was almost three months to the day after that night, and the first hints of fall were in the air. They didn't go anywhere near the place where Angela had died. And they didn't pause as they passed the playground. They did stop at Last Sam's cage, though. Neither of them spoke as they watched three little kids dashing in and out. One was pretending to be a lion, roaring the same way Eddie had done the first time he had gone inside.

They didn't talk much during that visit to the zoo. When they got near the stream, Eddie vaulted the fence and walked to the condo. He bent down and peered inside. It looked as inviting and safe as the first time he'd slept there. Nobody had been there since he'd left. The sleeping bag was still there. And the Swiss Army knife was still stuck in the ground exactly where he'd left it.

He looked around to see if he could spot the little duck that had become his friend for that time. But there were lots of brown ducks and he couldn't be sure. He hopped the fence again and he and Jack continued their walk.

It was the first time they had seen each other since Eddie was released from the clinic, and Jack asked how he was doing. Eddie told him he was back in school and that things were going okay. Steve had not come back and

Eddie's mother told him he was in jail somewhere in B.C. for assaulting a guy at a party.

"How is your mom?" Jack asked as they passed the conservatory.

"She's fine," Eddie told him. "She doesn't go to bingo anymore, but she gets out and does other stuff."

"You two . . . you doing all right together?"

"I wouldn't say we're best friends," Eddie answered. "Maybe we won't ever be like that again. But yeah, it's okay. Who knows, maybe okay is good enough, you know? At least for now."

"How about the life of crime? How's that part going?"

Eddie grinned. "I figured you'd get around to that. I'm so clean I squeak. I'm boring but clean. You reformed me."

"I didn't reform you, kid." Jack looked at him. "If you're reformed you did that yourself. All I did was find you a place to sleep at night and keep a punk from putting a knife in your guts."

Eddie knew it was a lot more than that, but he also knew there was no point in arguing. "How about you? You doing okay? You miss this place?"

Jack smiled. "I'm doing good. I got a different place to live. It's a basement suite not all that far from where I was. I figured I needed a change of scenery."

He turned to look at Eddie. "And no, I don't miss this place. I don't miss it at all."

They bought coffee and sat on a bench to drink it. "The first time you sat down beside me I figured you must be some kind of pervert," Eddie said between sips.

Jack nodded. "There are a few weirdos out there." For some reason they both thought this was funny, and they laughed for a long time.

When they finished their coffee, they walked some more, but neither said much. It was comfortable, just walking and thinking. When they got to the swinging bridge that Jack would cross to head home, they stopped and faced one another. Eddie noticed that Jack looked older. And thinner, too. Jack had never had a lot of bulk to him, but now he looked even smaller . . . *too* small. Eddie wondered if he was doing as well as he claimed.

"You ever feel like coming out to our place for supper, Mom says you'd be real welcome." As he made the offer he knew Jack would not come. "I told her about you. I mean . . . not everything, but she knows you're my friend."

"Well—" Jack held out his hand "—you've got a bus to catch and I'm heading this way."

Eddie shook Jack's hand and remembered the first time he'd done that. It was right outside Last Sam's cage. "I don't know if I ever thanked you for all the stuff you did for me . . ." Eddie's voice caught for just a second.

"No need."

"There's something I have to ask you."

Jack looked at him.

"How did you know it was me who broke into your house?"

Jack waited a while before answering. "Vietnam. When I was in the jungle, I figured out that if I was going to stay alive I'd have to teach myself to notice things . . . everything. After a while I got so if there was a branch bent at the wrong angle I'd see it. If the mud was swirled where it should have been smooth, or if there was a piece of root sticking out of the ground in a direction it shouldn't be going, I knew. Lots of guys didn't see that stuff and they came home in body bags. You made it a lot easier than the Viet Cong, believe me."

"The banana?" Eddie looked up at Jack.

Jack smiled. "That was part of it. I'd just bought the bananas that day and I always buy six in a bunch. I figured somebody comes into my house and doesn't steal nothing but a banana must be one hungry burglar."

They both laughed.

"I'll be seeing you, Eddie." It was the first time Jack had ever called Eddie by name. He smiled, then turned and walked away. It was a typical Jack Simm exit. As Eddie watched him go, he shivered, even though the day was warm. He had a feeling that this was the last time he would see Jack Simm. He couldn't explain the feeling, it was just there.

He thought about going after him, about trying to get him to come for supper today, right now. But he knew the invitation would just make Jack uncomfortable. Instead, Eddie watched Jack's slightly hunched back swaying gently in time with the movement of the bridge.

Eddie thought of another long-ago conversation. He didn't know why it came back to him just now, but it was there as clear as if the words had been spoken yesterday. It was the day of his dad's funeral. Eddie had been at the park talking to Mrs. Clara Campbell. As he watched Jack disappearing in the distance, he smiled as he remembered the last thing Mrs. Clara Campbell had said to him.

"Have you ever had a real adventure in your whole life, Master Slater?"

Eddie turned and began walking toward the bus stop. If anybody ever asked him that question again, he'd be able to say yes. He'd be able to say yes, all right.

Epilogue

February 26, 10:30 P.M. I never saw Jack again. I went by his new place, but Jack was never home. I left notes the first few times, but he didn't call. It was like he wanted to put that part of his life far, far behind him. I could understand that, at least I thought I could.

Only half a year after we made that last trip to the zoo together, Jack Simm died.

The funeral was yesterday. I went to it. As I watched the casket slowly descending to the place in the ground that would be Jack's final home, I thought a lot about the man who'd saved my life and changed it forever.

I didn't cry. I didn't really feel like crying; I'd done that when I first heard that Jack had died. The cancer Jack had for the last two years of his life finally overtook him. That was how the man who called put it. The man said Jack had given him instructions to let me know, but no one else.

Two years. I was surprised at that. Jack had been sick for the whole summer. And he must have known. Yet he never stopped doing what he'd done all those years. Every day he'd gone to the playground to look out for those kids.

I'll never totally understand it, I know that. There's no way anyone can know the guilt and the pain that drove Jack Simm to lead his life the way he did. And it doesn't matter. I figure what matters is that I will remember everything that happened last summer. For a while I was afraid I might forget some of it, that time would make some of it fade, like it does to a lot of things. But now I know that won't happen. I won't forget Ratsy or Jules or Stink Pagler. Or Linda Chen, even though I don't want to take her out anymore. I'll always remember the gorillas and the Siberian tigers and the Przewalski horses. Just like I'll remember the condo and the little brown duck. And seeing my mother that night at D.J.'s Bingo Palace and how it made me feel. I'll remember all those things. And I know for certain that as long as I live, I'll remember Last Sam's cage. Even though I heard it isn't there anymore. They moved it or tore it down or something. Anyway, it's gone.

Yesterday, as the casket came to a stop at the bottom of the rectangular hole, I was sure of one more thing, surer than I've ever been of anything in my life. I'll remember Jack Simm, too. Always and always.